New Life

#4: Correspondence

New Life

This issue is a special themed issue about correspondence. We asked artists and writers we know to reach out to artists and writers they know to see what would happen when they talked to one another.

To see all the ways people talk across distance? How we communicate and share intimacy and curiosity remotely? Maybe to get a sense of the things people are thinking about in their work or in their lives in all these different places? Something like that?

There's not really a huge, like, straightforward goal or hypothesis here. It's more like, let's put this out there and see what everyone does with it, and whatever everyone does with it will give us a sense of what it is. And become what it is. If that make sense.

Okay, thanks for reading. If you have any questions or

anything you'd like to share, you can send a voice memo to Wolfman Books founder, Justin Carder at 415-250-5527, and you two can figure it out.

New Life Quarterly is made by the entire crew at Wolfman Books. Tara Marsden is the profiles editor, Jacob Kahn is the reviews editor, Lukaza Branfman-Verissimo is the visual arts editor. Justin Carder coordinates a bunch of all of this. The magazine is designed by Justin Carder and published by Wolfman Books.

To subscribe or read pieces from previous issues, visit *newlifequarterly.com*

MI Leggett

+

Avery Trufelman

I went to summer camp with designer Mi Leggett. Back then, we were both kind of hippie-ish theater kids. I think we were in a production together that involved large paper mâché puppets? But it was a long time ago. It's funny that we've both got on to have careers that engage with fashion in different ways. I make a podcast about it, Mi designs it. I decided to reach out to Mi recently while I was in the throes of creating on my show, Articles of Interest, *to hear about what they've been up to, how their design process works, and why they make clothing at all.—Avery*

On Wed, Sep 5, 2018 at 1:45 PM Squarespace <no-reply@squarespace.info> wrote:

Name: Avery Trufelman
Email Address: ███████████████████
Subject: Correspondence
Message: Hey Mi,

This is crazy but we went to summer camp together at Interlochen! Wild eh?

I have been following your beautiful ascent from a distance and now, as a fan, I wanted to get in touch.

Now for my job, I make audio stories for the podcast 99% Invisible (www.99pi.org) and now I'm working on a spinoff series about clothing design (which will be out later this month).

This great local publication, Wolfman Quarterly (http://wolfmanhomerepair.com/books/), has asked me to reach out to a person of my choice and begin an email correspondence that they would then publish. I would love to be in conversation with YOU and talk about... I don't know, clothing production, presentation, growing up, etc? It could be just be a few emails. I know you're quite busy these days.

But mostly, it would be fun to hear how you're doing (are you still in touch with George DuPont or anyone else from back in the day)?

No worries if you can't swing it, but thought it was worth a shot.

Yours,
Avery
(Sent via Official Rebrand)

+++

On Sat, Sep 8, 2018 at 8:38 PM MI Leggett wrote:

Hey Avery!

Sorry for the delay getting back to you! I look back on my time at Interlochen so fondly and still distinctly remember a wild performance you gave lecturing about

2

Orwell's *1984* and dancing at the same time. Also, I'm still in touch with Keely Curliss! We ran into each other on an urban farm in 2010 when we were both working for the same sustainable agriculture non-profit, and continued to work there together for several years.

I'd love to catch up and have an email conversation. Ask me anything! Honored to be a "person of choice." Wolfman looks like a very cool publication and I love the idea of putting something so particularly digital into print.

Cheers,

MI

+++

Mi!

It's so lovely to hear back from you.

I'm so happy that you're game for this strange little exercise.

How bizarre to use email as the medium itself, rather than just the prelude to the actual phonecall/interview/meetup.

It's interesting: after our time at summer camp, we seem to have gone on semi-similar paths. You went to Oberlin, I went to Wesleyan (potato potahto, some would say), and then both went on to have a meaningful experience in Germany.

What brought you to Berlin? How long did you live there?

I studied abroad in Bavaria, but then fell in love with someone and lived in Berlin with them for a few months. Then I got a scholarship to go back for a few more months the following year. I vividly remember the only time I went to Berghain. I just impulsively decided to go at 3 a.m. and I wore my pajamas. I think I was so scared of being judged by the bouncer that I deliberately tried not to put any intention into my outfit, so that I wouldn't take it personally if I didn't get in.

Now, of course, I regret not dressing up for the occasion. I was so embarrassed to be dancing in my nightshirt, when everyone else looked so strange and beautiful. I kept meaning to go back again, but I think the fear of judgment loomed too large for me. That is a very un-cool thing to admit.

Do you recall your fist time going to Berghain? How often do you go out dancing?

Clubbing is such an interesting space, in terms of dress.

I have this little theory I have been thinking about: it seems to me that, historically, fashion was the realm of the disenfranchised (women, POC, youth, queers)—those who had no outlet, no megaphone but their own bodies. Now that we all have websites and social pages and other ways of being heard, the actual body is not the necessary canvas it once was. I feel like street style has become less important than Instagram style. Now we hardly need to have public bodies to have public style presences.

Except in places like music festivals and clubs. Where public life is re-engaged and looking is encouraged. These special conscious realms.

I might also be romanticizing this because I live in a city where every club closes at 2am. And the trains stop at midnight.

How often do you go back to Berlin? How do you split your time these days?

Yours,
Avery

+++

On Sat, Sep 15, 2018 at 7:16 PM MI Leggett wrote:

Hi Avery!

Happy Saturday. Sorry for taking my time with these questions. I love all these topics, I could go on forever.

I can't imagine anything better than being in love in Berlin. I'm so glad we both have been. Initially I was supposed to study there for a semester but I was so in love with the city and my friends there that I kept pushing my return date back and stayed for a year. Visiting last winter with my bestfriend/lover, Sessa, she told me she felt like she was home for the first time in her life, putting words to exactly how I felt when I first arrived.

She's back there now studying and I'll be there for some time later this fall. Long term, I'm planning to split my time between Berlin and New York pretty much evenly. Due to the unexpectedly rapid takeoff of Official Rebrand, sending me to Art Basel and New York Fashion Week(s) I've lived in literally ten different places in the past year, despite my plans for a low-key-post-grad year in Oberlin. After so much transience, I feel a strong desire to stay in one place (Brooklyn) but a stronger, conflicting pull to Berlin.

The first time I went to Berghain [bh] I didn't really know anyone. Once I was steeped in the community and culture however, I had much more fun—possibly the most fun. Bh and Berlin's queer party scene in general are exceptional places to embrace the full scope of emotions and expressions. You can really learn a lot about yourself through the intensity of the club scene. On the other hand, you can also take yourself away from yourself too. For me that lifestyle showed me a lot about myself, though of course at times I felt totally lost.

One of the most important parts of being in Berlin's queer art/party community,

6

was freeing up my self expression. I realized that the environments I had almost always found myself in had been really stifling. I grew up in a super preppy family, I went to prep school, and never really fit in at liberal arts college. I always struggled to conform to the expectations of those environments. My senior year at Andover (after studying away in Spain) I came back and was like, "Fuck this preppy bullshit," and I dressed how I wanted to dress and I didn't bother trying to fit in. But then I went to Oberlin where the social norms were totally different and it also took leaving again to realize how they weren't really for me. In Berlin I could be as weird and crazy as I wanted and be around other queer artists who truly excited and inspired me.

Queer parties are more than parties after all, they are political statements. Queers, who have been marginalized and erased can come together and express our full selves—that's not possible everywhere. These kinds of gatherings have been persecuted for ages and still are in many places. I never stop appreciating how lucky I am to have been randomly born into a time and society that accepts queerness and to have found spaces that celebrate it. Honestly it took me a little while to find those spaces. I remember going to straight clubs in New York as a teen and was just like, "Why don't I like this? I'm supposed to like this."

Back to bh though: The club's lore has become practically pop cultural because fear of rejection is something most humans share. Almost everyone gets rejected at some point. I've seen famous people get rejected. I know very few locals/regulars who haven't been rejected at least once. I guess it's good practice for everyone because life is full of rejections! I don't think its "un-cool" to admit fearing rejection. I do think its "un-cool" to be paralyzed by fear of rejection.

It's so funny that you wore your pajamas because actually pajamas and bathrobes have been pretty "cool" at the club circuit! If you are going to stay at a club from 8 to 48 hours, you might as well be comfortable...

Though I don't do it as much in New York, going out dancing is a really big part of my life and art practice. The intense stimulation of moving your body to loud music with so many other people—it's amazing. The simultaneous connectivity and isolation of the club provides a kind of sacred clarity and fertile grounds for growing ideas—which I have to immediately write down or they get lost in the moment. Clubs are also a great way to meet new people. Although it may sound superficial, I meet a lot of people based on their clothing. If I like how

7

someone displays themself on the outside, the chances are good I'll like how they are on the inside.

You could even say the same thing about Instagram style, it's just not limited by geography. I have friends from all over the world just from DMs. It's amazing that social media can break down these kinds of boundaries like geography. It's especially important for young queers who may not be accepted at all in the communities they live in but can find people like them online. I wish I had known the term "non-binary" in high school or that it was even possible to be a "they." Now kids all over the world have access to images and words of trans and non-binary activists/artists/models. Although, of course, access to queer culture should be more than just digital, it's a good gateway. For me, digital life is not substitute, but a supplement for our everyday experiences, influences, and inspiration.

XO
MI

+++

On Thu, Sep 20, 2018 at 11:46 PM Avery Trufelman wrote:

Hi Mi!

Now it is my turn to apologize for the delay. I've been in the throws of working on this podcast series about clothing and I feel like I have a mountain of things I want to ask you.

I so appreciate your effusive embrace of Instagram. There's so much to be said for appreciating technology as a bridge, rather than deriding it as some sort of false reality.

And that said.

I'm really curious about when and how you decided to turn to the business of fashion. When did you decide to really get a professional website and take professional photos and start to really invest in yourself as a brand?

Was it ever something you had doubts about? Was anyone in particular pushing you along or supporting you?

8

I feel like inspiration and creativity are the seeds, of course, but that kind of professional care and confidence are the water. And I don't know about you, but I find it so hard to remember to water my plants.

What is the next step for you in this regard? Do you feel a lot of pressure to come out with new lines? Do you have anyone assisting you? How do you turn a rapid takeoff into something sustainable? This is a question that might not have an answer.

I'm also curious to know how it has been experiencing THE Fashion World at Basel and NYFW?

Having never been within that sphere myself, I'm curious to know if you felt like you found your people within The Establishment. From the outside, I can't tell if fashion is the most radical place or the most conventional place, in terms of structure and hierarchy.

Oh, and I don't think I've outright told you yet how much I absolutely adore your repurposed jeans on your online store. Where do you find the materials to work with? What do you look for when you're searching for pants to revive?

Alright, alright, I'll stop peppering you with questions. Clearly I just want to get you a coffee one day in person.

<3

Avery

+++

On Tue, Sep 25, 2018 at 11:22 AM MI Leggett wrote:

I love your questions Avery! Though, of course an in-real-life coffee date would be lovely. Do you have any plans to visit New York soon? I just booked my flight to Berlin to spend much of the fall there and I could not be more excited, though I'm hoping to visit the West Coast sometime this winter.

I do really love Instagram but of course it has pitfalls. I try to focus on the bright side but social media can also be really alienating. It shows a constant stream of people and brands doing MORE—carefully curating and crafting their image. It's easy to compare my whole self to these constructed images and this can hurt because I am not a perfectly constructed brand, I am a person with flaws who experiences rejection sometimes. I try to keep these feelings at bay and remind myself that Instagram helps me more than it hurts me.

For me, the scariest part of social media is that it opens us up to jealously, which festers so easily. From my perspective, at least with respect to other young/queer designers I'm sometimes compared to, we are all working for a shared goal, helping people express their more authentic selves, so I prefer to tell myself that our success is mutual and not see ourselves as competitors, rather collaborators in making this world a more visually exciting place where people are more free to express their true selves. I know that is super idealistic but it is way more productive to think positively than enviously.

No matter the mindset I bring to it, if I spend too much time rubbing my phone I start to feel weird and bored. But I do try my best to keep in mind that posting my own stuff has been essential for getting my work out there and getting feed-back on what I've been making.

Not long after I started posting pictures of clothes I was defacing, friends and strangers started hitting me up to make stuff for them. ATM gallery in Austin asked me to ship them pieces for a pop up shop and I started to realize I could make a thing of it. Though my personal ig handle was already @official_rebrand I actually planned to call the label "offbrand" because I love knock-offs and I was thinking a lot about authenticity/fakeness in fashion and identity. I realized quickly that Official Rebrand was actually a much more fitting name. In 2017, I registered it as a business and got a website, etc. On the verge of graduation, the idea of being able to do what I actually wanted to do as my means to sup-port myself provided serious motivation.

Of course I had doubts. Like many about-to-be-college-grads and recent col-lege grads, I often felt overwhelmed by a sense of impending disaster, but so far, my life/career since graduating has surprisingly exceeded my wildest expec-tations. Now I just try to keep so busy that I don't have time to contemplate the possibility of failure. This is probably why I am so bad at meditation.

Besides keeping busy, the other major part of taming my fear of failure is my amazing partner in life and crime, Sessa. We met in the Tank Co-op at Oberlin about a week after I got back from Berlin. Distraught about leaving Germany and my friends there, I repeatedly showed up for meals with sunglasses on so no one could tell I had just been sobbing my face out. One thing that cheered me up was this tall sparkly beautiful person with weird clothes that I liked a lot. Within a few weeks we declared our love for each other and a few months later we smuggled her illicit ball python to come live with us in my student apartment.

At the time, she was just starting to get into photography so we started shooting together on this white brick wall right outside my apartment. It felt organic and symbiotic (and hot). We compliment each other so well as collaborators and our partnership has been integral to growing our individual art practices. Sessa's unwavering love and support has really made it possible for Official Rebrand to be what it is and for both of us to be who we are today. For me, she is both seeds and water.

Now about getting things done and watering plants:

I try really hard to remember to water my plants because apparently they purify the air and my paint has formaldehyde in it. I also keep a huge to-do list and am pretty diligent about promptly crossing off the things related to my business while the personal health and wellness ones tend to linger. I have been meaning to go to the doctor to refill some prescriptions for over a year now…

Regarding next steps, now that I've written it here, I promise to finally get around to scheduling (and showing up to) that doctors appointment. Regarding Official Rebrand, yes I feel a lot of pressure to keep producing work at the rate I have been or even faster. I think it might be healthy for me to take the next year to go a little slower and really figure out what direction I want to go in and who I want to collaborate with. I mentioned before the "unexpectedly rapid takeoff" of my label—and the truth was, I was planning to take it pretty easy for the first year after graduating—but opportunities came up to show at NYFW and Art Basel and various pop ups so I never really got the rest I was planning on.

It's unlikely that I'll actually take a real break anytime soon, but I'm trying not to put too much pressure on myself and to create at my own pace. Thinking long term, but getting things done one day at a time will probably be the only way I can make this life sustainable.

One of my major goals for 2019 is to have a gallery exhibition, as, in addition to clothes, I make a lot of sculptures and large scale paintings on sheets and blankets. I've noticed that as a young person, it's a lot easier to sell T-shirts than paintings on king size duvets, but that isn't going to stop me from making both.

I have friends who are incredibly supportive and encouraging, but no assistant

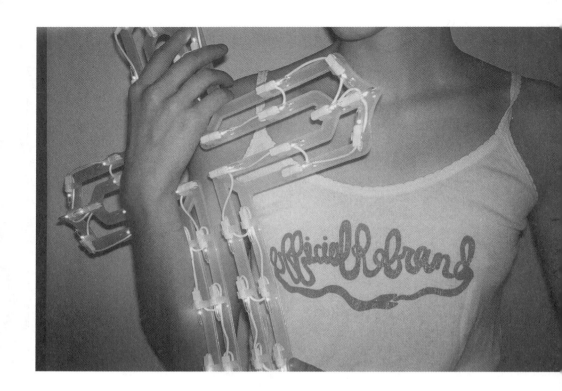

at the moment. That's another goal of 2019. If you know anyone who you think would be a good fit, let me know!

Honestly, I might not be the best person to speak on THE Fashion World anywhere. Because my project is mostly about rejecting the social and industrial norms put in place by the fashion industry, I feel somewhat like an outsider. I'm making a brand that rejects traditional notions of gender and consumption and proposes alternatives that oppose what the fashion industry wants us to think.

I do enjoy being a voyeur in the fashion world though. I LOVE seeing people dressed the fuck up, pulling wild looks—fashion events can be fun for that. I try to always bask in my appreciation for looks I'm into and express affirmation as much as possible—it really gives me life! I don't think people really go to fashion parties to have fun but I do my best to make them fun. Once at a Berlin Fashion Week party Sessa and I rolled up with several baguettes our friend Rosa was about to throw away at her bakery, The Bread Station. Sessa went around using the french bread as a sword to knight people, including Peaches. We definitely got some looks.

But of course there are amazing looks to be seen outside of "the fashion world." These are the ones that often inspire me more. I find looks that are not steeped in whatever is currently trending are often more original and raw. Often the most original looks come from those who aren't paying attention to what everyone else is wearing or what trend forecasters are focusing on. So, I try to keep my eyes open wherever I am and really try to maintain my passion for fashion, even if I'm not super smitten with the industry side of it.

According to friends who work for more established brands, the pressure is cutthroat. When I grow my business more and take on a full-time team, I want to challenge those norms as well and have it really be like a family. Food is super important to me (after years of working in sustainable agriculture) so I'd want to make communal cooking and meals a big part of my company's culture. If you are going to be working with people all the time, it might as well be fun.

I'm so glad you love the water jeans project! Most of the jeans come from friends or family. Sometimes I buy them at thrift stores. I have learned it is a lot more fun buying jeans for other people based on color/style as opposed to searching for a pair that fits me.

If you send me a pair, I'd love to rebrand them for you! <3

XO

MI

+++

On Wed, Oct 17, 2018 at 2:54 AM Avery Trufelman wrote:

MI!

Hello hello!

My deep and sincere apologies for the delay. I was finally, at long last, releasing this podcast series about clothing and organizing our celebratory afterparty fashion show. Oh I SO wish you could have been there to show your work on the runway (that we built with our bare hands. What a crazy thing).

15

Anyway, that's no excuse—we're all very busy in this world. I'm sorry for the radio silence.

But in the aftermath of this podcast, everyone is asking me if I will do a second season and it's anxiety-inducing. It's so lovely to read your words, and to remember that even if rest is nowhere in sight, it's good to try to take things a day at a time.

Well, here's to painting on king-sized duvets and gallery shows and living it up in Berlin! Thank you so much for your generous responses to my rando questions. I have to send this correspondence off to the magazine soon—but before I do, may I ask for any pictures you may have of your process? Happy to just pull from your Insta if you dont have any readily available—but I would love to see some images that you wouldn't normally post on social.

I'm giving a talk at SVA in February (I have no idea yet about what) and I'll be in the city for two weeks. I would love to say hi in person.

May I seriously take you up on your rebrand offer? I would looooove that. I have been thinking a lot about water and denim for the episode I did about blue jeans and I would love to wear that statement proudly. Thank you so much for offering that—that's so kind!

Let me know your address and I can mail you goodies from Oakland (and a copy of the magazine!) as a thank you.

It's been so utterly delightful to catch up, Mi.

Yours,

Avery

+++

On Wed, Oct 17, 2018 at 2:54 AM Avery Trufelman <averytrufelman@gmail.com> wrote:

So glad to hear you are coming to New York in February!! Please come over for dinner and bring some jeans for me to rebrand.

I have loved your rando questions and can't wait to read the whole magazine!!

Also, a very cool thing about *Articles of Interest*—my friend sent it to me to check out after the second episode aired and I was very happy to see it was in fact the podcast you have been working on! I love it. I am such a ho for history and love hearing about the history of all these aspects of fashion—and the stuff about children's clothing. So weird!!

Here are a bunch of pictures!

Can't wait to get together soon.

XO

MI

Kwame Boafo

+

Dongyi Wu

I met Kwame in 2015 while he was getting his masters in Intercultural Communications in Shanghai. He later traveled to the southern city of Guangzhou for his research thesis on socio-cultural relationships between the Chinese and Africans that went beyond the political and economical space. Drawing from his experience in Ghana and China, Kwame's art practice has been engaging on topics around marginalized people, social identity, gentrification, colonialism, race, gender and capitalism, and centers the idea of the body as a vessel of historical memory.

For Kwame, "the colonial body suffered brutal inhumane deeds." His work searches for an opening for the body to [re]member these lived experiences and create counterforces to resist contemporary forms of oppression, making the body an author of resistance strategies.

We communicated via text on Whatsapp over a period of two weeks in October.—Dongyi

*Photo: Abdul Arafat @abdularafat_*

Dongyi: I remember meeting you in 2015 in Shanghai through a mutual friend, when you first started living in China. It was a serendipitous encounter for me, having lived in Accra in Ghana for five months during school, and then meeting you in China, when you began your research into the African community in Guangzhou. I partially went back to revisit my hometown to learn about the African community that grew there, to learn and understand how this community exists in relation to Chinese society. My time in Ghana back in 2010 was the first time I realized how China's economy was extending beyond exports to the West and how it has been steadily gaining influence on the African continent through trade. I was also very amused to learn that most of my Ghanaian friends grew up watching a beloved Chinese classic on television—*Journey to the West*—about a monkey, a monk, a pig, and a pilgrim. I'm curious what you've learned during your time in China and some of the more memorable experiences that have influenced your work.

Kwame: China has been a big part in my art practice and research. Coming to China was the first time I was leaving the shores of Ghana and it has been quite an experience for me from cultural shocks to researching into Chinese relations with their African neighbours in Guangzhou.

My practice started, for the most part, in China and this began as a result of my quest to move beyond language or text for want of a better word. At the time, I felt during every performance (mostly text based drama) the emotions and spirit of the text were lost in translation and so I needed to find a language that is not text based. Also I was searching for a language that can be created during the period of the performance together with my audience. Also, we felt well-made narratives often make people think in a certain direction which are mostly guided by their prejudices. We (myself and my Bulgarian friend Yassen Vasilev whom I met in China) co-created a performance that explored the limits of the body. This was my first non-representational, non-text performance—although I observed that the movement vocabulary was developed as a reaction to various text and articles by renowned philosophers. We developed my first

solo performance "Nutricula" which was the first performance of "In The Flesh," a series of live performances at Minsheng Art Museum. Shanghai was a serendipitous moment for me as I find out how the body can be used as a tool for storytelling, how it has been deprived of its own story, and how the body says things that words cannot.

Also, living in Ghana my entire life and hearing stories of how people live in glamour and joy outside the continent and being confronted with a sharp contrast of the living conditions of the people in China, hearing and seeing the various oppressions and atrocities that people go through was also a marker of influence.

On countless occasions the racial aspersions and slurs that were thrown at me or others around me made me question on a daily basis what it means to live as a Black body in our era.

Again, the rapid rate at which high rise buildings were springing up at every moment in every nook and cranny in Shanghai was also a marker of influence as it made me question what happens to the memories of the people who had lived in these places—will they suffer historic amnesia? What will be the inter-generational narrative of the place among others?

So yeah, I accumulated lots of experiences in China and these have become bookmarks that I draw from in my works.

Dongyi: Can you expand more on how you've been using the body as a tool for storytelling? What does/did it mean to live as a Black body in China, as opposed your experiences in Ghana, or the UK?

Kwame: There are so many energies that flow through the body and it manifests itself through tangible and intangible means (i.e. emotions, facial expressions, physical actions, movements etc.). My work as an artist is to allow the body to move through space as it [re]members its lived experiences and connect these energies. Oftentimes in my work, the body leads in the narrative and presents a tapestry of movements that immerse it in a physical and visceral dialogue between the body parts. This is the way the body speaks and it breaks patterns and delves into the unknown.

The complexities and challenges that came along as a Black body living in China was overwhelming and a minefield for me. Initially, it was fascinating how my colour became my immediate identifier/name as I heard on countless occasions "hei ren lai le" (a Black person is coming) when I passed by. This was not so much of a surprise because growing up we had also called out white people whenever we saw them in our community.

My negative experiences included people sometimes walking out of elevators whenever I get in, people not sitting close to me in the train, people covering their noses whenever I walked by. The most hilarious one was when I was asked if I see tigers all the time when I'm in Ghana. That was an awakening for me, because it was a reflection of what the media shows—which is the narrative of Africa being endowed with great flora and fauna. There was also that part where I had to take on an accent or demonstrate beyond reasonable doubt my mastery and command of the English language before I could be offered a job. Living in China, there was always the "you don't belong here" narrative that almost glaringly stares at me all the time. After a while I got Chinese acquaintances and we had great experiences, connections and conversations. It makes me question the initial repulsive attitude towards me as a Black body; was it an unwitting naiveté or a pervading racial bigotry?

My lived experience in Ghana is unlike these experiences; my colour has never been my identifier. I would rather be called "chale" which literally translates into "buddy." This is a daily reference and marker of belonging. In Ghana, there is always a sense of home despite the complex and numerous socio-economic problems we go through.

My recent visit to London gave me mixed feelings. I went there to work and also be part of a theatre festival, and I'm glad I got the opportunity to experiment in a non-conventional space and show my practice and research to a new audience.

It was fascinating seeing firsthand the enormous social transformation in the city. All I could think of at times were people living off the residue of the enormous resources pillaged from the continent. I immediately started thinking about reparation and how it's long overdue. Also, almost every Black British person I heard talk revealed how the system is made to their disadvantage and the daily struggles they go through. I could make connections with the spill overs which manifested itself in different ways in China.

Dongyi: Thanks for sharing your experiences of being confronted with these challenges constantly. The misrepresentation and ignorance about Africa and Africans in Chinese media can be so absurd it's almost surreal. Unfortunately I think the combination of the legacy of Western colonialism and imperialism as well as media representation that dominates the narratives of Africa in China continually perpetuate terrible stereotypes which prevent Africans from finding belonging in the country. I'm interested if your explorations in non-text/movement work can be a bridge to this gap.

Kwame: I forgot to mention that my Chinese teacher once asked me in class if we have high rise buildings in Ghana and we were talking about development. She was also quick to point out that pictures and news from the continent constantly show kids with flies and running noses, not having clothes or shoes on, head bigger than body and all. That becomes a bookmark for indexing and interpreting development within the African space. I couldn't blame her especially because these are the alternative pictures about the continent aside from the flora and fauna. So it became difficult to engage on that level because already her mental pictures and prejudices are sourced from a weaponsmith (Western media) that believes in keeping the Black race perpetually out of the discourse of development.

It actually forms one of the reasons why I went into movement performance. What I realised again is that there is prejudice about African dances being energetic and aesthetically elaborate. So I decided to look at the fringes of these markers and present a performance that will not feed into the narrative. I remember after one of my performances a Japanese friend came to me and was like, "When I read that a Ghanaian and a Nigerian are performing, I thought it was going to be a beautiful dance but no, you guys talk about serious issues, it was dark and too much for me." So immediately you see you've deflated their Expectations 101. Now you can have a genuine and proper conversation on the performance. So, yes I saw movement performance to be an avenue to create a vocabulary that is not tainted with imageries that links my mostly Asian audience with the existing narrative.

Dongyi: I find that oftentimes when artists and performers from non-Western countries are showcasing in Western places and institutions, there are unspoken expectations to perform the culture—and in your case

24

there was an expectation for you to do that with African dance. How do you contend with drawing from your lineage and history while also creating beyond those limitations? Were you ever challenged about whether your work is "African" or "Ghanaian" enough?

Kwame: It's actually a great feeling to ruin or dismantle an audience's expectations with my performance.

All the subjects/thematic issues that are brought to bear in my performances are sourced from my immediate environment and the history of my lineage. I give vivid representation of the sentiments, aspirations, challenges of my lived realities. I also feel the complex content of my historical and contemporary life are forcefully represented in my work.

There's a recurring statement I hear whenever I speak about my work: "We need to preserve the culture." Meaning the culture of my parents' generation or even beyond them. I mean it's great to

*Abdul Arafat @abdularafat_*

be aware of these cultures and apprise them at all levels because it forms a part of my identity—but then again identity in this global space is moulded around a complex quagmire that goes beyond territorial cultures.

So I find that statement a bit tainted in the sense that our new realities are equally our culture, and we invariably become vanguards in preserving them and it has to be demonstrated through our works as artists because our art mirrors life.

Also I feel we need to move beyond the "exotic" and nostalgic feeling that these cultural performances are made to evoke.

Dongyi: I completely agree that we have to go beyond exoticization of cultures and allow free exploration of artistic manifestations. However I also see the necessity of continuing the practice of certain traditions because they give power to groups who have migrated or been displaced from their homelands, and for me I'm thinking specifically of immigrants and refugees in the U.S. whose sense of identity and community is helped by these cultural performances. What comes up in mind, then, is who is the performance intended for?

I'm also curious about this topic because I have had my own journey grappling with wanting to be viewed beyond the color of my skin growing up in the U.S. and have actively downplayed my cultural heritage—but at the moment coming to a place of seeing my peoples' history and lineage as complex and nuanced and using that as a springboard for my artistic practice.

Kwame: I'm also curious to know what necessitated the need to actively downplay your cultural heritage growing up. Was it the environment you found yourself in at the time dictating it, or it was it a conscious effort by you to sidestep your own cultural heritage?

And do you now view the culture you're assimilated into as foreign/hollow/etc, hence the need to retrace your steps—"Sankofa" as it's called in the Ghanaian Akan setting—to find your complex and nuanced historical culture?

I believe that by all means we need to apprise ourselves to our cultural heritage, we need to continue its performativity. However, it shouldn't be cast in dogmatic terms so that it ends up being a restriction. The thing is these dynamic cultures open themselves up to adapt to the ever changing times. I feel (and this is just a feeling) that if we get ourselves saturated in cultural dogmatism we may end up losing out on the evergreen realities of our time.

I draw from traditional Ghanaian ritual as an initial source of energy for my performance and that's a way of connecting with my traditional lineage. And so, we cannot, and should not, think of obliterating these cultures—that would be ridiculously bizarre and naive to go on that path. I'm actively learning and unlearning ways to present stories from the continent, but I'm also careful it doesn't get consumed by

27

exoticisation. That becomes a distraction and opens a new conversation that I am not interested to participate in at least for now.

Dongyi: As someone who migrated to the U.S. as a child it was a difficult transition coming to a foreign land where many things I've learned that were perceived to be normal became weird and undesirable, so I felt a social pressure to assimilate and be accepted in some sort of way. I now see that my cultural heritage also informs the way I've learned to see the world, the way I interact with my blood family and my people, and I want to understand that. My desire to connect with my culture and ancestry has more to do with my own process of dismantling white supremacy, that was pushed onto me in order to survive. So now I'm in the process of unlearning this part of myself and attempting to understand the places from where my lineage flows.

With that, I want to hear more about the concept of Sankofa, and how you draw from Ghanaian rituals for your work.

Kwame: Sankofa is an Akan word which literally translates into "Go back and take."

San: To Return

Ko: To Go

Fa: To Take

Its pictorial symbolism is represented by a bird with its neck fully turned back taking an egg while its feet face forward. It is forcefully used to open up conversations on reflecting on the past in order to shape the future. We believe that the past must be a guiding light in our pathway to securing the future. As we seek to create new knowledge systems, we must always take cognition of the past.

The word was used, I believe, during the transatlantic slave trade. As many of the slaves were believed to be from West Africa, slaves who ended up in the New World constantly reminded themselves of the need to return to their homeland and ancestry. This was generation-

Nii Kotei Nikoi @NiiKotei

ally inherited and it served as a reminder to return.

Also, after independence, it became a quotidian word that was used by the newly independent Ghana to remind herself to return to the knowledge systems and codes that her forbearers used before colonialism came in and forcefully tried to exterminate and replace them. It's also a way of reminding Africans in the diaspora of the need to return to their ancestral root.

It often comes with the proverb: "Se yen were fi na ye san kofa a enkyi." Which can literally be translated as, "If we forget and return to take, it's not wrong."

As an artist learning and unlearning ways to decolonise my practice, it guides me in retracing and researching my existence. However, one must be guided in order not to ignore/obliterate the present culture/lived realities.

Performance for me is sourced from our daily ritual and ceremonies. The Ghanaian trajectory of life is marked by various ritual performances from child birth to death. These performances serve as an immediate point of reference for me as an artist. My performance also seeks to reach out for the innate primate sense of self to find organic movement vocabularies that serve as an arsenal for the body to tell its stories. The body is a repository and author of anything and everything organic. My aim is to explore the metaphysical (that which is unspoken, seen as a taboo) dimensions of human experience to arouse a visceral resonance.

Paul Mpagi Sepuya

+

Mitsuko Brooks

Wolfman,

I mailed you a typed up letter tucked into a mail art piece early this morning that could potentially function as text describing the project, or not. In reading over the text messages slowly, I began to hear Paul much more clearly and am rethinking our entire mail art correspondence. I assumed Paul was too busy so I realize I told him directly to not mail me anything in response, although he was completely willing. I'm becoming more aware of how I naturally am creating an echo chamber by keeping my mail art one-sided. Selfishly, I assumed if I was the only one sending him mail art then the show at Dread Lounge would be a solo show. The more I think about this correspondence project I begin to see that it is not a solo show, and that it is a two-person show (even if Paul did not/does not send a photographic response). His presence was necessary for the entire project. Without him there would not be a unique correspondence and no show, as he had invited me to use the space. I only now also realize Paul was interested in the participatory aspect of this process and willing from the very beginning most likely due to his life commitment to the pursuit of art. I realize I stonewalled something really spectacular that could've happened. Additionally, I am left confused as to who actually owns the artwork. I need to create a disclaimer prior to beginning my future mail art correspondence project.

—Mitsuko Brooks

Sunday, August 26, 2018

Dear Paul,

Hope you are doing well! Congrats on your upcoming European solo show! I had one of your grad mirror pieces at my old bedroom in Altadena — and my cat was playing around and knocked it over. It went crash! and now its shattered in so many pieces, it just feels wrong to throw out the pieces — i might try and repair it with cement...

So anyways — i got invited by my mail art collaborator hika2a branfman-verissimo to submit a mail art correspondence to new life quarterly — to document and print how artists build communities — capturing discussion of work, i want to ask your permission and interest for me to use the first four or so of these pieces as part of the project, as mentioned, we can fuzz out your address, but you're pretty famous — so i understand if you are not interested.

Art life is pretty exciting! I feel like all these exciting things are happening — I want to hold tight and ride this wave without getting too stressed, someone (i don't know who) contacted ST gallery to buy postmarked older mail art works from me, I found 2-3 ones mail art letters from 2009 — 2014, written from my old chinatown apt in NY, to an ex boyfriend, etc, — and i reread them and it made me sad and confused to sell them to a stranger who doesn't know any of these people — i'm thinking about the intimacy and sentimentality of them — and how its so strange, they would be bought for 600 and i would get 300 for them. I'm broke and need the money so im gonna sell them but ask for more than 600, i've never felt so attached to my art work before. Its interesting!

Love, Mitsuko

Mon, Aug 6, 10:03AM

Mitsuko: Welcome back to LA & congrats on your upcoming show!!! I think I want to send you mail art from now until the show, is that ok? I'll discuss my ideas for the show in the work. What is Dread Lounge/your mailing address for studio? Xo

Mon, Aug 6, 11:17AM

Paul: Oooo cool. I'm heading home to LA tonight. There's no mail receiving at the studio but you can send to [redacted]. Is that cool?

Hope it works conceptually.

Mitsuko: Oh yeah totally as long as you don't feel uncomfortable with your address being exposed. I have also blurred out people's addresses when using images in the past.

Paul: Oh trueee maybe we just blur or obscure it?

Mon, Aug 6, 2:17PM

Mitsuko: Yes

Mon, Aug 6, 8:33PM

Paul: Super. Glad that works! Can't wait to see what develops!

Sorry I'm bad at typing lol

Mitsuko: Awesome!!!!

Mon, Aug 20, 9:23AM

Paul: back in town and got the first mail piece. it's beautiful. should i respond by mail, or do i gather and hold onto them until we start install? i am going to get all the info on the dread lounge space from [redacted] this week. Wishing you the best with the move to Little Tokyo, and wonderful to hear how positively the service center has been through everything. [heart emoji]

Mitsuko: Yaye! You can just gather & hold onto them. If it's not too much of a burden to ask you to scan & email the first few to me that would be super helpful. I'll tell you why in my next piece. I'm sure you are crazy busy so I can also meet u at your studio to scan the first four or so to scan myself. Xo

Paul: scanning them will be super easy! should i wait til there's another 2 or so?

Mitsuko: Yeah!
Thank you Paul! you are amazing!

Thu, Aug 30, 12:29PM

Paul: Another one just arrived!

Mitsuko: Wow!

Paul: So i just have to track down where the sign up sheet went to and find out who's doing the october and december shows and we have to figure out the logistics w them directly

Mitsuko: Cool!

Paul: If we can't find it this week will email the building to track it down

Thu, Sept 6, 10:04PM

Paul: I just got home to find the next mail art piece. Thank you! I love it. The typewriter and the delicacy of the paper on the bookboard. Will scan the group so far tomorrow and set up a google drive w everything.

Mitsuko: Cool! No rush

Paul: Shall i send the floorplan of

40

Dread Lounge? I found the info on the schedule, its up to us to contact the folks showing in Oct and Dec to arrange our dates and stuff

Mitsuko: Oh yes please

Paul: [heart on envelope emoji] its so nice getting your pieces in the mail

Mitsuko: Ok I can email them if you want and just bcc you

Yaye! So nice to hear!!!!!! Hope you are doing well!

Paul: And i know that feeling about storage AND the experience of replying to someone with your work's price and not hear back

I'm ok. I started keeping a notebook and journal again to sort thoughts. Was getting deeply stressed. It helps a TON

So things are gonna be A OK

Mitsuko: Yes! I'm doing the morning pages and it helps so much.

Yes they are.

Paul: I hope work eases up to give you more time for art work

Mitsuko: I hope you find less stress. Yeah I'm finding a balance. I'm also itching to go to nyc in October so I'm excited about that plan

Paul: Thanks! You too. What are your october dates?

Mitsuko: I haven't got them yet but after the 15th I think

Paul: We'll just miss each other there then!

Mitsuko: Awe! Darnit

I can mail you a preemptive mail art to get while you are in nyc if you have your friends address?

Paul: Ok i will see who makes sense.

In nyc briefly mostly in providence and new haven and new paltz for talks

Going to amsterdam Sunday if you wanna send something to FOAM fotomuseum by next friday

Mitsuko: Ok I'll do that yaye!

Wed Sept 26, 6:49PM

Paul: Do u need the pieces scanned before we meet?

Or can we do in a couple week?

Im making rough scans have never scanned non flat things

theres a fucked up background in them all i cant get rid of

Maybe they can be retouched

if you want to

Or you can try again

Mitsuko: I can retouch em it's my specialty!!!

Thank you Paul!!

Just a few are fine.

Wed Sept 26, 10:55PM

Paul: Ok, One sec, i uploaded them all

Sun Sept 30, 10:40AM

Mitsuko: Dear Paul! Thank you for these! The editor (Lukaza Bran-fman-Verissimo my mail art collab-orator) wanted to indeed include these in New Life Quarterly Magazine published by Wolfman Bookstore in Oakland. I wanted to double check you are ok with this (with your address blurred out of course). Would you be interested in including a response to these pieces/if you are too busy I can send you screenshots of your texts for approval? I understand if you are too busy/not interested.

Paul: Hi! Yea do use them. I could maybe make a photo response?

Mitsuko: Oooooooh yes! I'll photo-shop & send you for approval first. And a photo response would be glorious!

[END OF TEXT MESSAGES]

42

Ra Malika Imhotep

+

Jasmine Gibson

Dedicated to Ntozake Shange
(1948—2018)

two writing-ass blk wimmin connected via email to discuss our relationship to drapetomania—"the disease causing negroes to run away." one a mental health practitioner. the other phd student. both drawn to poetics as a medium of articulation. both kind of into black women performers in vintage porn. both curious about the other's work.—Malika

Peace Jasmine,

....For the sake of introduction I'll start with a brief disclosure of how I came into this piece ("Hysteric Drapetomaniac" in *The Black Aesthetic Season II*).

"Hysteric drapetomaniac" came from a real personal place of me grappling with my own mental health realities and how I kept seeing them mirrored back to me in the blk wimmin creators I held close to my heart (Nina Simone, Ntozake Shange, Lauryn Hill, to name the few I was thinking about early on). I began to wonder how my hypomania and my crying fits might be a product of inhabiting this unconquerable "metaphysical dilemma" that is "being alive, being a woman, and being colored."[1] Then just sitting with myself and my work (as a doctoral student in black studies) I was reminded that the desire to be free and black had been historically constructed as a mental illness and that to be a woman with feelings had also been diagnosed as mental defect. Yoking the two together made sense, I felt oddly at home in-between these made up labels. I literally wanted to print stickers and put them on all my things. To mark myself as part of this tribe I had made up by appropriating these racist and misogynist constructions. This desire to be free of something that was not my blackness or my femmeness but the structures that made it so i couldn't see mysel(ves), couldn't be whole. And these were all winter daydreams. Then the semester started and I was taking a course on Black performance theory and I found myself back there. I wrote a thing. And then unwrote it with more room for lyricism. And that's what was published in *The Black Aesthetic.*

My first questions—where did you/do you find "drapetomania"? What do you hear when black folks say the word crazy?

+++

Hi Malika,

I'm so sorry I'm late to respond. I've been thinking about your prompt. I don't really envision anything concrete in what form this conversation will take but I'm excited to explore that with you. I see what you mean about holding space for the Black women and yourself in the historical ways in which the foundation of

---

1. Ntozake Shange, for colored girls who have considered suicide/when the rainbow is enuf (1976)

LADY ERNESTINE
EXOTIC QUEEN

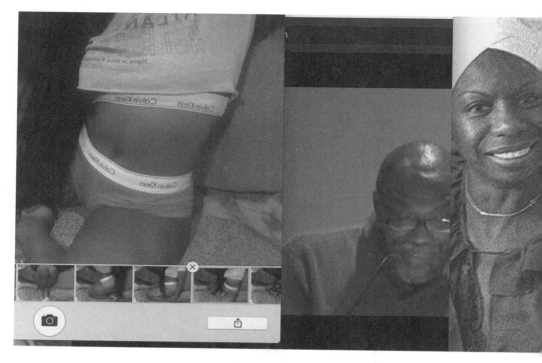

race and the psychiatric begin to form in the new petri dish of the Middle Passage and the Americas. There's a certain "madness" to the process of racialization, it's the feeling of being quartered and confined to an existence that you've "walked into" but the conversation is always changing around you and you need to "keep up."

How I came to drapetomania was from a historical materialist perspective first, because of my politics and seeing how the Black Women in my own family dissociate or imbue the other Black women in my family with this ennui of anxiety, which is necessary for operating in the world as a Black woman. Then I came to understand drapetomania in work, thinking through the work of feminist theorist Hortense Spillers and Silvia Federici, when I worked as a case manager in the Bronx, and now as psychotherapist in Bushwick. I then started to think about this in theory pieces I wrote. I titled my chapbook *Drapetomania*, because I was thinking of the historic allostatic load that is inherited when you are a Black woman, and trying to explain that in poetic form.

Most of my patients are black and women, and they say "crazy" all the time, and I recognize that as a means of people trying to grapple with the immaterial things they've received from the world. When they say crazy they mean "instability" or "being unable to grasp" onto something stable that's been placed out of range for them by external determinants. I see it as a starting point in order to talk about how emotional and and psychic vulnerability has been weaponized to discredit people, particularly other people that look like them and me. It's an opportunity in the exercise of political education.

My question for you, what stood out for you with the

piece (the antebellum Black lesbian pornographic photo spread that appears in "Hysteric Drapetomaniac")? Is the weaponization of contact feigning for intimacy or is that what it is at all?

+++

hmmm. "grappling with the immaterial things they've received" really resonates with me.

getting into the porn piece requires [another] bit of self-disclosure. I initially encountered the images as a tumblr post that has since been taken down. the blog was called "retro-fucking" and basically just shared images from vintage porn spreads. I think the first thing that caught me was the juxtaposition of lesbian desire and antebellum iconography. a lusty aunt jemima. so before I even confronted the obscenity, the pejorative, I was wrapped up in fantasy. Treva Lindsey and Jessica Marie Johnson have an article, "Searching for Climax," which is kind of interrogating how (black women's) pleasure is rendered unimaginable in the time of slavery and subsequent freedom. And i think my initial encounter with the image was very much me, this black woman in the isolation of her own bedroom engaging something I couldn't believe had been thought up, performed, and captured. I tracked the image down, found the exact issue of *Hustler* they were published in and ordered it. The hard copy (complete with musty basement smell) kind of sullied much of the liberatory possibility the images held in my imagination.

Hustler was/is a notoriously crass pornographic publication. The tagline for the issue in question was "nothing is sacred" and there were several "nigger" and "jungle bunny" jokes peppered throughout the publication. Even the language given to contextualize the photo spread was a far cry away from the story the images told me that one night on tumblr.

But following some really paradigm shifting work on black sexual economies—L.H. Stallings's *Funk The Erotic*, Jennifer Nash's *The Black Body in Ecstasy* & Mirelle Miller-Young's *A Taste for Brown Sugar*, Ariane Cruz's *The Color of Kink*—I was working to hold space for the models in the shoot to be performing their own work and to hold space for my own erotic imaginary which meant allowing the things these images in isolation communicated to me to be valid and taking my gaze and all its black queer femme particularities seriously.

I wanted to read the images in a way that willfully displaced white phallic fantasy, so it wasn't really about responding to the weaponization, but wanting to say something along the lines of, "The images are meant to stimulate and while I may not be of the number imagined in the initial production, by naming the thought they stimulate in me I am reclaiming a bit of what the framing of this encounter inside of my history is meant to falsify."

I'm curious about your thoughts on the relationship between pleasure and mania. The erotic, the pornographic and the real. Thinking back to someone like Nina Simone whose insatiable sexual appetite is often discussed in a kind of unannounced parity with her mental health struggles. As a poet, as a professional, do pleasure/the erotic/the pornographic move anywhere (together or separate) in your work?

+++

Hi Malika,

I like how in your previous email you describe how you found the images. I am a bit of a fan of vintage porn, especially with Black women performers. There's something interesting about how Black women were framed at that time. Where you see a reckoning of the Black Power Movement kind of pushes this sexual and powerful Black woman to the front that isn't on the front of a colonial card or joked about being raped. This Black woman is sure, she's celestial, she's hot and cannot be touched. It also produces a lot of vulnerability in the image of the Black woman. I think personally I like these images because in some narcissistic way I see my own body shape. My favorite is Lady Ernestine, she was a

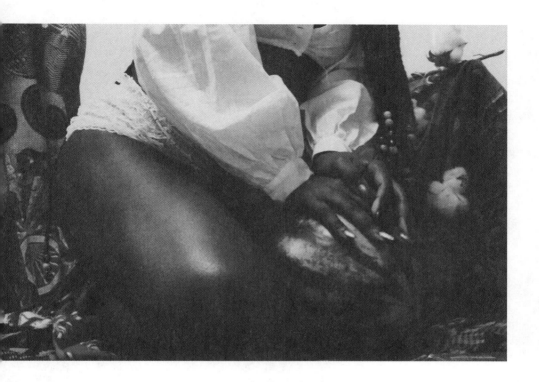

burlesque dancer, and there's this beautiful picture of her with a boa and I think she became a body-builder.

Anyway, I think that on the flipside of this, magazines like *Hustler* took advantage of that and wanted to distill this more well-rounded take of Black women and sexuality to recenter it into the Jezebel during slavery looking for a fuck. Which is a white phallic fantasy where the agency of Black women is still under the heel of white masculine sexuality. Because outside of that view Black women are seen as objects that are just inflicted upon. Golems meant to awaken to a master's call.

How I see this professionally is the lack of sexual education in Black and Brown communities. There is very little conversation about Black and Brown people actually enjoying their bodies, and understanding what they want emotionally, sexually, or psychologically from relationships. Conception is discussed as a punishment. Someone like Nina Simone is interesting to think about with her

own sexuality because she was often demonized and pathologized for it. For Ms. Simone, what could've been seen as "oversexualization" could actually be seen as a negative coping mechanism that she had available to her. And particularly in her life, she was in an incredibly violent relationship with her husband where deprivation of personal freedoms, like having an actual place to feel physically and emotionally safe—of course you're going to be seen as "oversexual" because it's probably the only thing you do personally that makes you feel anything at all.

The erotic and pleasure are pretty prevalent in my work. I think they are prevalent because I thought there couldn't be pleasure without pain, so I endlessly

sought out pain to get pleasure. I was, and probably still am, inspired by this Bobby Womack quote: "Sly Stone once told me, 'Bobby, you fall in and out of love faster than anyone I know.' I live for love. I've always been tortured by love. I don't mind the pain. I want to be the king of pain."

I've been proven wrong by that hypothesis and can love without pain. But I think that's the challenge of wanting to love in this world as a Black women—wanting love in a world the doesn't want to see you or believe you are worthy of love.

Mary Welcome

+

Nicole Lavelle

I heard about Mary long before I met her. We had similar orbits on the DIY residency circuit and an insanely intricate web of mutual friends. "Do you know Mary?" People asked me this everywhere I went. I think it was because we have similar handwriting.

We finally met in January 2014 in Green River, Utah, which served as Mary's home-base for four years while her housing in Palouse was heartbreakingly precarious. I was back in Utah for my fourth annual visit, to make a project with my friend Sarah Baugh and Epicenter. We all proceeded to fall in love with each other. (I have the commemorative stick-and-poke to prove it.)

I wonder sometimes why my deepest friends come from the same network of itinerant visiting artists whose practices engage place and community. I guess it's because we find it easy to relate. You haven't been home for four months either? You want to talk about the ethics of narrative extraction, too? Lucy Lippard is also your favorite? You also want to take the longest possible route to get to where we're going? Okay. Friends forever.

In the five years since we met in the winter desert, Mary and I have found ourselves together in Maine, California, Washington, Idaho, Oregon, and probably somewhere else. Only this year did we visit each other's homes. We are each other's favorite houseguests because all we want to do is work.

We're working together on a project about, for, and with visiting artists that still has no name, and whose form is morphing as we add pieces to it. We're both maximalists, we both just want more, more, more. We relate in that our creative strategies are accumulative.

We've thought so hard about what it means to be a visitor, a local, a guest, a host. We're trying to put it all to words, and this interview is the latest layer of that thinking.

Our correspondence took place inside our favorite in-browser collaborative note-making product from a file-sharing company, because we support each other in the goal for less email. —Nicole

Nicole: You identify as a citizen artist. What does that mean?

Mary: I think the term citizen implies a greater accountability to the place and the people. I did a project in Minnesota a few years ago about celebrating citizenship and wielding community force by taking ownership of the term "citizen" on a neighbor-to-neighbor level rather than as dictated by people in power. I think that citizenship is something earned and awarded through care and stewardship of place, and something we should generously bestow upon one another. Feelings of belonging, you know? The power of belonging that begets great care. This is a pledge I wrote for community citizenship, it applies very directly to my practice and process as an artist as well.

> AS A CARD-CARRYING CITIZEN, I PLEDGE TO:
> - Nurture the strengths of my community and work to alleviate the weaknesses
> - Treat my neighbors (human and environmental) with compassion, cooperation, and respect
> - Communicate about problems with a willingness to take an active role in finding solutions
> - Donate my time and my talents to improving quality of life in my neighborhood
> - Set healthy boundaries and be aware of my limitations
> - Enjoy and celebrate this unique place I call my home
> - Take care of one another

Tell me about your encounters with difference in your work. Is it a necessary part of the work? Is tension required? Do you have specific strategies for

navigating tensions of difference? I'm thinking specifically about tensions like urban/rural, insider/outsider, local/visitor, past/future…

I'm not sure about the terms of difference or tension. But I do think that variables, unknowns, autonomous zones, and in-betweens play an important role in my process. Undefined spaces in places and in relationships often are the most productive ground for creative thinking, problem-solving, digging deep, and transformation. I spend a lot of my relational practice working to draw community members together in new ways/venues, in order to establish veins of solidarity that relationships can grow out of. So maybe it's more about water-witching for compassion points, rallying moments, and unity energy—and knowing that I can lean hard on those powerful hot spots in order to navigate difficult differences.

So much of being a good artist is being a good listener. Because of this, I often feel tasked as translator—visually, linguistically, intuitively, creatively. I spend a lot of time in communities with my ears open, repeating back what I am hearing in order to better understand and to illustrate. I think the best way to respect difference is to model not only good listening practices, but also soft confrontational practices. Empathetic inquiry, conversational research, casual didactics. When we can have our conversations with an emphasis on our shared human-ness, we can be more sensitive to one another's life experiences. I've learned so much from folks who were willing to meet me somewhere in the middle and walk me to their side of a story. What's the difference anyways between a long walk and a long talk? Slow strides. Soft power.

You and I write and talk a lot about the dispersed network of place-based, itinerant, engaged citizen artists that we're a part of. You've also called it a "network of accountability" and described "resources that exist across time and space." Can you describe this network? Who's in it, what do they do? How is its dispersed nature part of its intrinsic value?

I do a lot of pretending to be a Luddite, but the truth is I'm pretty grateful to live in our twisted high tech connected world. So much of my work wouldn't be possible without online documents and video calls and eternal email inboxes. The ability to keep communicating with the people in places I've worked—no matter the weather and time zone and mileage (and in spite of my slow rural broadband internet speed)—is integral to doing the work that I do. That being said, I'm a big believer in slow-talk too, and do plenty of letter-writing and postcard sending.

I think more than anything that being able to work remotely (on the internet) and on-site (real life person-to-person hanging out) has helped with the persistent lonesomeness that comes from the kind of live/work migratory practice that I have. I've got to be ON and FRESH and STOKED in every place I go to, I'm constantly a newcomer, I am almost always tired. There's so much of fatigue that sets in from going it alone and working at getting people together. If there's one thing the internet has taught me, it's that there's more of us than I thought. We're out here in the hinterlands, hauling across the country, sending emails in dawn's first light from mobile car offices, meeting folks for beers at the VFW— and we can reach out, touch base, check in with one another. I've met so many practitioners that can relate to the delights and complexities of an itinerant locational creative practice; heck, I'm in more collectives than I can count, for sake

I ONCE TOLD A LOVER I COULD NEVER LIVE IN THE EAST AGAIN BECAUSE TIME PASSED SO DIFFERENTLY THERE. I AM QUITE FOND OF VIRGINIA, THE NORTHERN NECK ESPECIALLY. I HAVE A FAMILIAR, EVEN FAMILIAL LOVE FOR THE TREE TUNNELS AND CREEK BEDS & THICK UNBEARABLE BLANKET THAT IS SUMMER TIME. I FELL IN LOVE WITH THE OLD AMERICAN HIGHWAYS WINDING AROUND AND LISTENING TO STORIES OF SUCH A WORN-IN STATE. IT WAS VIRGINIA THAT TAUGHT ME TO EXPLORE SLOWLY, TO TRESPASS WITH AN ALIBI, TO LOOK CLOSE AND LISTEN CLOSER. TO TREAT YOUR MEMORIES WITH THE SAME TRADITION OF SOUTHERN HOSPITALITY. TO KEEP YOUR SECRETS, HOLD YOUR GRUDGES, REMEMBER TO FORGET. TALK TO YOUR NEIGHBORS AND AT LEAST NOD TO EVERY CAR THAT. LONG DRIVES GIVE ME THE SAME FEELING AS A LONG EVENING... A FRONT PORCH. THOUGHTS HANGING IN THE AIR LIKE FIREFLIES. ON & OFF, ON & OFF. MORSE CODE MAYBES, WELL I NEVERS, NEEDLESS TO SAY TIME GOES IT'S OWN WAY. EMPTY HOUSES CLING TO THEIR SECRETS, ALL HEMMED IN BY KUDZU AND A WILDERNESS THAT'S TRAPPED INSIDE, WILD-IN-A-CAGE FEELINGS I GET THERE. OLD STORIES SHIFTING UNCOMFORTABLY BENEATH THE FLOORBOARDS. ALL THE HAUNTED SPACES, PLACES— DUE TO MEMORIES MORE THAN MY OWN. SIC SEMPER TYRANNIS, HOLD YOUR HEAD PROUD, AND A QUIET FIT SCREAMS WHEN THE RAIN POURS DOWN ON A TIN ROOF, SUMMER STORMS ON THE POTOMAC.

NICOLE LAVELLE
211 CORTLAND AVENUE
SAN FRANCISCO, CA 94110

of working harder with more people power and better conversational critique and counsel.

I meet people in the places I work in, I meet people at conferences and convenings, I meet people on the internet. (Nicole and I know each other from the internet, first. Letters later.) We stay in touch. It's a proactive long-range slow motion game of catch. In the same way that I need this dispersed digital community to help keep me critical and transparent, woke and stoked—I rely on that same community to do mutual lookaftering, remind each other to drink water and stretch, offer perspectives from their distant time and places. The shared experience of SHARING EXPERIENCE is one of the best tools in the network toolbox, by staying in touch (with work, with life, with projects, with feelings), I can constantly reframe, gain new perspective, connect people and places to more people and places. Grow the circle of friends.

Speaking of dispersed networks, let's talk about the U.S.PS. Tell me about God Bless the U.S.PS. Why is the United States Postal Service so important? What values does it represent to you? I get it: I also have an active correspondence practice; you and I have sent mail back and forth for years. You exhibited a correspondence project between us at a solo show in Calgary. Recently we each dropped $100 on deadstock stamps at a barn sale in Idaho. What were we thinking?! What's the draw? Why postage, why letters, why postcards? Is it nostalgia? Is it a physical embodiment of connection?

The U.S.PS is so important. Simply put, it's the last shred of a communications commons that we have as a nation. I'm everyday blown away by the fact that you can send a message, a protected private message, hand-to-hand across this **entire** country, for fifty cents. What a world we live in. It's an accessible, noble, romantic, highly functional, ready-steady miracle of an institution. Don't be fooled; email doesn't belong to you. It's not private and you need an expensive machine to make it work. Your words written and sent on paper though, that's yours and ours and worth fighting for. We need to work together to protect our right to communication.

It's a risky and generous thing, to sit down and put pen to paper, and give it to a stranger, who will give it to another stranger, and another and another and another, until it reaches someone you care about. Sometimes that's the most comforting part. I spend time daydreaming about how my letters end up in the homes of my friends; it makes me feel real and glad and alive. And a little bit magical.

You live and breathe in Palouse, Washington, but your work takes you far and away. Is leaving a necessary part of feeling at home? Do you feel like a multi-centered person? (Shout out to Lucy Lippard.) Has your attitude towards multiple centers changed throughout your life?

I don't know if leaving is a necessary part of feeling at home, but leaving sure keeps me nimble and humble and happy to be home when I am so. Home in Palouse, that is. I grew up with a really fluid definition of home, home as an action, a making of a safe space, a together place. Homing as verb has always rung truest for me. I've recently re-acquired a book of stories I wrote between kindergarten and second grade and I carry this poem around in my heart when I am on the road and feeling homesick.

Last spring we drove from Lagunitas to New Cuyama, and what is typically a four-hour drive took us 16 hours of driving over two days. We stopped in Monterey to visit the army house you lived in with your family for a few years and you wondered to me about the impact of your itinerant childhood on your art practice. You said something about the feeling of living on base, how there was always a process whereby you felt welcomed. Can you remember some of that? Can you re-explain?

Living on military bases, you're surrounded by people who are moving around all the time. There's a sympathy for strangers, rather than suspicion; people tend to be really gentle with one another about the leaving and the going and being the new kid over and over again. I remember so many welcome loops, ways to reach out and say hello to neighbors, how to see and be seen, how to create feelings of belonging for one another. It's the simple stuff that my practice is built on—potlucks, block parties, dropping in, taking walks, returning phone calls, writing thank you notes, babysitting at the last minute. There's a sort of radical hospitality of open invitations and pitching in and following through

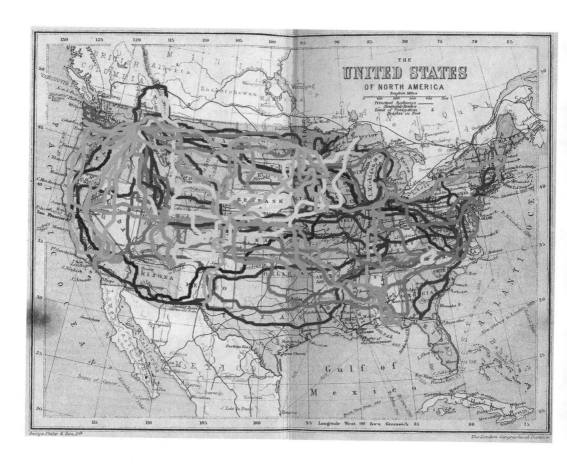

that's just the day-to-day ethos of living on base. Everybody's from everywhere, everyone is homesick for somewhere, and we're all buying the same groceries from the same commissary; we all felt a responsibility to build healthy community in our temporary neighborhoods.

It's definitely been influential in my practice, and a reason I spend so much time thinking about how to be a good visitor, a good houseguest, a good artist-in-residence. In a strange way, being a visiting artist feels a lot like moving around in a military family—figuring out how to make earnest, thoughtful, helpful actions in a new place, often on a tight timeline and a shoestring budget. How to tread both lightly and diligently. How to be careful with community. How to feel familiar and familial.

What is challenging about living rurally? What stereotypes are true? What do you hope will change over time, and what are you working to change?

Something that is really difficult about living rurally is visibility. I live very publicly in a very small community of 900 people on the Idaho/Washington border. There's no public transportation to where I live, it is very far from any interstates, it is nowhere near Seattle. I live there on purpose for lots of reasons, but an especially important one is that I'm not interested in working autonomously as an artist. I like to work deeply and reliably and I chose a place that holds me accountable and models intentional community practices while at the same time accepting me at face value as the growing, changing, flawed human person that I am. I moved to Palouse about 13 years ago (when I was 22!)—I've moved through so many different versions of myself during that time, with the gentle affirmation and counsel of an entire intergenerational town, made up of a spectrum of folks I never would have had the opportunity to befriend if I lived in a city. Palouse is a promised land to me, a place I won't grow out of, a place that wears me in instead of wears me out. It is nice to be seen and looked after and cared for and challenged and included. So much more is possible when your humanity is validated in an everyday way.

On the flipside of that, choosing to intentionally live and work in rural communities across the country excludes me from "the scene"—that ever-changing urban-normative network of funding and opportunities that thrives in and near metro areas. Outside of my direct network of itinerant rural cultural workers, I often feel totally invisible, especially as an artist. Most days, I'm frustrated and scheming on a shoestring for how to continue to do my work in the kind of places that matter to me. I believe that artists belong everywhere, within the entire rural-urban continuum! Every community has a right to cultural resources and creative vision and everyone ought to be able to choose to live in the kind of environment that they thrive in. I used to say "You gotta live in a place that loves you back."

Back in 2015…how Heather and I met:

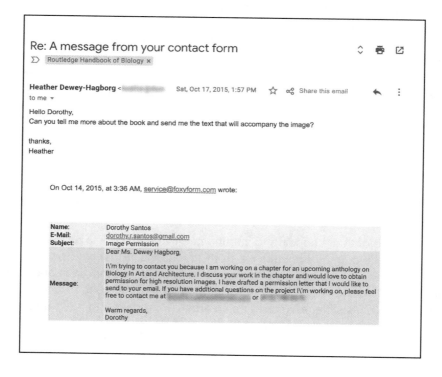

Heather Dewey-Hagborg

+

Dorothy R. Santos

In 2015, I was granted the opportunity to write a chapter for an anthology about biology in art and architecture. In my research of artists using bioma-terial as a part of their practice, I found Heather's work. A few years prior to our meeting, she developed Stranger Visions during her artist residency at Eyebeam. She collected human detritus found on the Brooklyn streets and created computer generated portraits she turned into 3D printed masks based on DNA phenotyping. I was enthralled with her work and needed image per-missions since her work was on the artworks I wrote about for the anthology. As someone I deeply admired, I was nervous. You never know what to expect when contacting an artist you admire. But we exchanged email messages, got the permissions, and subsequently met in Point Arena, CA the following summer and we instantly connected. Since then, we've been collaborators for REFRESH, which is a curatorial collective she founded in 2016. Despite our distance, Heather is one of the people I correspond and speak with frequently (actually, we correspond in some way/shape/form multiple times a week, if not every day). She has lovingly become my work wife. A true long-term relation-ship that spawned from overlapping intellectual, societal, and cultural interests and passions. I've learned a lot and it's been wonderful getting to know her professionally and personally through a multitude of channels.—Dorothy

EXCERPTS OF DIALOGUE ON
GENERATIVE REPRESENTATION

Heather: Is forensic DNA phenotyping a photographic process?

Dorothy: Are you drawing distinctions between photographic processes based on evolutions of the apparatuses? Basically, I'm wondering if you have thought about specifying further. For instance, "is forensic DNA phenotyping a digital photographic process?"

Heather: This is indeed a good question. I was considering photography broadly, as an expansive post-digital practice.

+++

Heather: You can essentially drag an algorithmic slider to make a face lighter or darker, more male or female, etc. according to the parameters and limitations of the underlying model, and characterized by the data that determined the model in the first place.

Dorothy: You have discussed this previously, but the "algorithmic slider" seems to add a subjective and unreliable aspect to the overall process.

Heather: Yes. This is so clear when you imagine a slider concretely between any two things (i.e. how can you make a face more male or female, for example, when

Assigned to
Heather Dewey-Hagborg ✓

Dorothy Santos
5:13 PM Oct 13

Are you drawing distinctions between photographic processes based on evolutions of the apparatuses? Basically, I'm wondering if you have thought about specifying further. For instance, "is forensic DNA phenotyping a digital photographic process?" +heather@deweyhagborg.com

Assigned to Heather Dewey-Hagborg

Heather Dewey-Hagborg
12:59 PM Oct 16

this is indeed a good question. I was considering photography broadly, as an expansive post-digital practice.

Today I would like to explore a different aspect of this technology, one that has not been widely discussed, which might begin with the question, is forensic DNA phenotyping a photographic process?

67

HD
Heather >

Yes you are welcome we have lots of food!

No problem

Just come eat with us:)

I'll try and get there as fast as I can. See you soon!

Fri, Oct 12, 9:03 AM

We are middle apt

Are you close?

Yes

Here

Coming

Fri, Oct 12, 2:30 PM

Spoke with Josh

11:45

HD
Heather >

Tuesday 12:15 PM

ok i emailed 😊

if you want to chat for our interview thing im here

Wednesday 12:08 PM

hey 😊 are you available to talk to hyphen tomorrow morning? I'm in flight unfortunately

at least they replied 😃

Yes! I am available in the morning. After 11 am PST. I can repose to their email.

Great!

Today 10:20 AM

hey there

there is so much variation within these categories?) only by creating a reductionist stereotype. You could think about eye color this way also. What would a slider for eye color look like? Irises are so incredibly complex and often have multiple colors at once.

+++

Heather: With a more detailed technical understanding, now let's return to the question of whether phenotyping is a form of photography?

Dorothy: I feel compelled to ask you what you think of Karen Barad's notion of agential realism? Essentially, coming into being through what Barad considers "intra-actions" and something always becoming. Also, I am struck by the tense of the word "phenotyping," which alludes to something always changing with "ing."

Heather: I haven't read about it! Send me a paper :) Interesting point on the "ing" making the phenotype active—it does indeed highlight that it is a human activity, not a given fact in the world. That it is a process of construction.

+++

Heather: In a time of science, capitalism, and democracy, representation was everywhere.

Dorothy Santos
5:16 PM Oct 13

You have discussed this previously, but the "algorithmic slider" seems to add a subjective and unreliable aspect to the overall process.
+heather@deweyhagborg.com

Assigned to Heather Dewey-Hagborg

Heather Dewey-Hagborg
1:02 PM Oct 16

yes. this is so clear when you imagine a slider concretely between any two things. i.e. how can you make a face more male or female for example when there is so much variation within these categories? only by creating a reductionist stereotype. you could think about eye color this way also. what would a slider for eye color look like? irises are so incredibly complex and often have multiple colors at once.
Show less

Thus you can essentially drag an algorithmic slider to make a face lighter or darker more male or female, etc. according to the parameters and limitations of the underlying model, and characterized by the data that determined the model in the first place.

Dorothy: Before scientific advancements with genomic research, phenotypes, the visual were the things people had to go by and make assumptions on and think through. So, now, contemporaneously, genes and blood become the new medium for political agendas (we discussed Elizabeth Warren in my race and genomics class yesterday!)

Dorothy Santos
5:33 PM Oct 13

Resolve

I feel compelled to ask you what you think of Karen Barad's notion of agential realism? Essentially, coming into be through what Barad considers "intra-actions" and something always becoming. Also, I am struck by the tense of the word "phenotyping," which alludes to something always changing with "ing".

Heather Dewey-Hagborg
1:03 PM Oct 16

i haven't read about it! send me a paper :)
interesting point on the "ing" the making phenotype active -it does indeed highlight that it is a human activity, not a given fact in the world. that it is a process of construction.

With a more detailed technical understanding now let's return to the question of whether phenotyping is a form of photography?

Thanh Hằng Phạm

+

Jeannine Ventura

Hằng & I met at an audio making workshop they were co-leading in Los Angeles called Sound Bodies. We've kept in touch via email since.—Jeannine

Sat, Aug 18, 10:03 PM PST
Hi Hằng!

Regarding the Sound Bodies workshop and how it was healing: it was interesting because my partner and I in the workshop got to discussing the sketches we worked on to indicate sounds. When I got to thinking of the intersection of bodies and sound, I got to thinking about the noises fat bodies make and those living in larger bodies. I thought of how sounds signified taking up space and existing and how as a fat femme this was often a sight of hypervigilance, body dysmorphia, shame, paranoia. I was always afraid of taking up too much space or the over-creaking of a chair, breathing too heavily, huffing, etc. It was illumination on the ways even sound can marginalize or police certain bodies.

+++

Wed, Aug 29, 9:16 PM PST
Hey Jeannine,

Thanks for sharing with me your healing experience. That sounds powerful. Sound workshops like that are healing for me too.

I'm having a tough mental health day…one of those days where my body just feels raw. Burying myself in work seems to help me from getting sucked into a vortex. I made a radio doc on the weekend about my mum and I, and I think I'm feeling the effects of it now. When I woke up I was thinking about internal sounds, "loudness" in the world and sound footprints. I'm such a sound nerd.

I'm hoping to move overseas next year—at least for two to three years. Either somewhere in Southeast Asia or NYC. Both feel like similar places to me.

+++

Aug, 30, 2018, 12:35AM
Hi Hằng,

Sometimes we are left with what we're left with even when we embark on projects that, to others, may seem like they'd bring healing or insight. Sometimes the digging and the looking back and into and deeper gets romanticized. It calls for so much and takes so much and we give so much. So much is conjured too.

What motivates this move? What do you find yourself daydreaming about re: location?

+++

Sep 1, 2018, 5:14 PM PST
Hey lovely,

Yep, it's so easy to romanticize the "digging deeper" into a feeling or a project, and social media has this weird but not surprising way of glorifying every emotion.

The story is called "27" and it's about the limits of motherhood in the face of adversity. (FYI—there is content of domestic violence.)

In terms of moving, yeah, it's exciting! Nothing concrete (no plane ticket yet), but working towards it feels good. Melbourne has always been home, always will be. In ways I am so lucky to have grown up here with solid connections to some family members, grow up on land where First Nations people have been very vocal and active here in Narrm (Melbourne). But now I really want to try the challenge of living somewhere else and learning to build from the ground up again. Sometimes I think social media makes me feel like I know everyone already…and I don't like that. Social media has been amazing to connect with other queer POC diaspora folks, but I wonder what connections could be made outside of that. What's your relationship with Instagram? Right now I'm gonna take a bit of break from IG because I see myself moulding into someone that others can "like." It's weird.

Sep 10, 2018, 11:20 PM PST

(TW—mention of body dysmorphia, eating disorders, trauma, etc.)

Hi Hằng,

I listened to "27" as well as other stories like "Gravel Road of Love," and "When I Loosened My Grip." Your work is stunning! Thank you for inviting me to your private, familial, ancestral and painful stories. I love the way you work with sound. Your stories made me travel. It felt like a dream or soundscape as well as a story. There is such beauty and realness there. I can't speak boundlessly and irresponsibly about the beauty of your work without acknowledging the immense pain there too. Particularly with "27." What has been the aftermath for you? How does it feel documenting this and evoking those memories, stirring spirits and emotions? We did touch on how difficult it can be and how that work isn't all that it is cracked up to be in practice. It isn't always life-changing or freeing or liberating.

I noticed how there are similar patterns (as in the rest of the world due to colonization & imperialism) of settler colonialism and oppression in Australia and the U.S.A. (of course with important distinctions) but the similar notes are hit and a cadence emerges. How does it feel to have grown up in a place (Narrm or Melbourne) as a queer child of the Vietnamese diaspora, a non-white person, in a settler colonist state, on First Nations land? What was your journey and education like when thinking on and coming into yourself in these contexts?

As far as social media—I hear you! For me, it is so complicated. As someone who has a lot of social awkwardness and anxiety, it has been both good and bad for me. On the one hand, when my depression and anxiety is too much to take and I do not leave my house or my room, it is a way I can speak to people and still feel like there is a world out there. I have made friends around the world and I cherish those relationships. The other side of it is that, well, it can become an obsession and a tool that encourages and enables avoidance, comparison, and posturing in me. I sometimes find it becoming yet another method of isolating myself. It also becomes a tool by which I bludgeon myself. I often use other people's carefully crafted and curated stories and feeds on as a way by which to measure and devalue my own experiences, accomplishments and life. It erodes at my mental and emotional health. I'd love to learn to balance my use of it.

I recently saw a story of yours wherein you were very honest about your body dysmorphia & history with E.D. Thank you for sharing this. I know the journey to realizing our past issues is non-linear and quite messy. No neat bow or happy ending in sight. I very recently have started to realize that I went through disordered eating and excessive/obsessive exercise for most of my adolescence and young adulthood. Unfortunately, due to the fact that I've always existed in a fat or "plus size" body (though there have been times I was on a thinner point on that spectrum) my issues were never on healthcare professionals', teachers', or my family's radar. My rapid, erratic weight loss was applauded or overlooked due to toxic diet culture.

I'm particularly interested in hearing more about the origins, development, production and intention behind Mình. I am so struck by the fact that the heart is not the core of the body/being but rather it is the stomach. Wow!

+++

Sep 11, 2018, 5:29 AM PST
Jeannine,

My motivation to keep working in sound is about connecting with others (near and far) and maybe in some sense it makes me feel less alone. I also think that there is so much room to play around with this medium—from podcasts, to sound workshops, to documentaries and so on. I have had a couple of people, including yourself, reach out to me about "27" and some other radio work I've done. People sharing their own experiences and it is so precious. If my work can give people some meaning or feeling in their life then it's worth making something.

What inspires you to keep doing the work you do? How do you stay true to yourself and your practice? I have yet to really develop a practice, to be honest.

Regarding my history with E.D….yes, those reflections have been coming up lately because it's been a year since I was in a very difficult place. I was in a toxic intimate relationship and had a toxic relationship with my body. Grief is definitely not linear. There are still some "sounds" and movements in my body that remind me of that difficult time. I hope one day I can really free myself from those reminders or at least learn to calm them.

I am definitely in a better place but I also am trying to make space for the little things that creep up every now and then. It frustrates me that our society upholds toxic and narrow beliefs around food and bodies. E.D.s among people of colour are definitely misunderstood and I want to keep having conversations with people about it. I would love to hear more about your experiences around E.D.s if ever you want to share. I'll listen.

+++

Sat, Sept 22, 2018 1:42 AM PST

I've been thinking about Hiroshi Yoshimura's *Green* album you and Jessica played at the top of the Sound Bodies workshop. I've been playing it for the plants in my home. I've been thinking on the communication styles, intelligence, and social networks of plants. I forget they're alive and intelligent. I also have been thinking about the intricate or diverse ways we communicate with each other and the world around us. What we're listening to and what we're not or can't even perceive.

I've always struggled with taking up space in the world, expressing myself verbally, and feeling comfortable with myself and my identity. Writing has been something I've loved doing ever since I was little. I couldn't draw, I couldn't sing or play an instrument, I was terrible with numbers and all things logical (to this day as well). Writing was always something that came so easily and was the only thing that felt right. I could explore painful, deeper, beautiful things and process them through writing in ways I could never otherwise. Still do. I haven't been writing much lately. I have a habit of denying myself things that are good for me or that I derive joy from. Without avidly reading, my writing tends to dry up.

Undertone was born from frustration and loneliness. I always wanted to put other POC on while creating on my own terms. Luckily, I met other women who felt the same. We are pretty much aligned in our goals and intentions for *Undertone*. I am motivated by trying to create a space where folks can tell their stories and learn to expand their creative capabilities. All while prioritizing womxn and femmes of color in a nurturing environment. I want to learn how to better amplify these voices and perspectives.

How important is community to your work? I think community is integral to my work, whether it's *Undertone* or if it's my other side projects. The few episodes I have recorded for my podcast are all featuring guests from my friend groups, community, or internet friends (I actually need to edit all that raw audio. I've been avoiding it, as I do most things). All this work is created in community. Folks submit their work to *Undertone* Mag. It'd be nothing without their sacred work. The *Undertone* collective team works together to produce, publish, print, promote and distribute the publication, together.

I don't think I mentioned that I'm trying to resurge my novice oral history collection for CLRJ's Speaking Story project. Do you take oral histories? What

importance do you think oral histories have? Any tips for gathering oral histories? I learned some tough lessons from my mistakes thus far and this project has been dormant for a LONG time. I want to start this endeavor up again! I need to. Wow, I guess avoidance, stalling, and stasis are common in my life. The CLRJ Speaking Story project is created in and for community. The histories are stored for posterity in an archive and they're derived directly from the community. It's a way to get at history, direct from the source, gathered from the community itself. It's a way to capture unspoken or undocumented experiences that often get obscured, ignored or denied in dominant historical narratives. The lives and experiences of womxn, femmes, gender non-conforming people of color and marginalized folks. I don't know where to start again. With yet another thing, I feel lost.

I don't know how I stay true to myself and my practice. I don't know where to even start. Everything is in process and nascent for me.

Well, I've been highly insecure lately. I've started a new job. It has potential but, I find myself floundering in professional environments, per usual. The trauma and unresolved issues really do overlap into all relationships and aspects of our lives, don't they? Even in professional spheres. I can kind of already feel the self-sabotage creeping in and it shows. Recently, I've been thinking about work and my trajectory and my future. I kind of panic at the thought of it. Also, I'm finding waking up harder and harder. Often, the first thoughts I have in the morning are quite dark and a little hopeless because I get to thinking about how plan-less and directionless I am. I stir awake with a pang in my stomach and a nervousness, anxiety flaring in the early morning. I feel as if I've wasted time with no navigation or destination. I feel out of options for some reason.

I've also been thinking about legacy, lineage, family, familial history, ancestors, culture for some years now, the older I get. There have been a few milestones and medical situations occurring in my family over the years. I feel so disconnected from them—they're in southern California. At first, I created this distance through my obligations, now I choose to have distance, in a way. Time and their lives have progressed without me, as they should. But in many ways I don't know them. I am not a part of their lives. Little ones are so much older now and I don't have a presence in their lives. I don't offer them comfort or guidance. Elders are aging and falling ill. I am not there to care for them, love them or listen to their advice, experiences and perspectives. Those are all finite resources and gifts that disappear once their vessels and carriers pass away. I feel like I am losing time and connection. Who am I without them? How will the stories and essence of my family be carried on if time is not taken to capture them? I've been wanting to record my family's oral histories for a while now. Due to my distance (physical and emotional) after all these years, I feel mildly estranged and like a fraud if I tried to re-integrate into the fold.

I wonder what is the link between sound and pain or trauma? It is ok that these difficult sounds and movements still exist. It is ok to not be ok. We are so solutions- or answer-oriented in our culture, that liminality and the long, hard, complicated process of healing or processing is overlooked or rushed. I think, exacerbated by social media, there is such a focus on the "glow up," on the Before vs. After, on achievement. This is so prevalent in toxic diet culture or self-improvement culture, for example, due to capitalism and the cult of positivity. It's even permeated our emotional/mental/spiritual well being too. This obsession with linear progression and "coming out the other side" better or wiser or more "well rounded" can stunt us from actually feeling what we feel, on our own time. There is no end destination. But striving for one is ok as is wanting to be able to control our emotions. Sometimes, I do feel overwhelmed by how comparison, competition, and linearity has even infiltrated personal healing and growth. What if we don't want to, cannot, or won't heal. Is that ok? I think it is. I think it is ok to exist with liminality. The liminal in many ways and expressions interests me.

Regarding food and bodies: Well, it is complicated. I seem to be developing mild forms of agoraphobia this past year. I think it is definitely linked to my moods and mental/emotional health but, most of all, it is linked to fatphobia I experience often. It has led me to kind of hide. I'm not proud to say it, as we live in a culture where the cult of positivity and the marketable, somewhat vapid and narrow #bodyposi perspective has taken over. But this is the reality. Fat folks and people with "unruly bodies" (as Roxane Gay would say) don't have the pleasure or luxury of simply "loving themselves" out of marginalization, aggression, and oppression.

+++

Sunday 14 October 2018 10:56AM (AEST)
Hi Jeannine,

I feel some deep shifts happening as well as a need to keep going. I'm thinking about what it takes for us to connect deeply to ourselves, be our very most and help our friends, family and community to be their very most without being sucked up in capitalist and ableist ideas around "proving yourself/productivity." Navigating your new job, do you think all these feelings about ancestors has come up for a reason? For me, everytime I go through a shift in my life what happens is I get a bit fixated on what's happening on the surface (conflicts with people, my upset feelings, frustration, etc.) and then I eventually realise that there's deeper work to do.

I used to think that distance was a barrier, but lately I am seeing it as a bridge—a door, an invitation to change something (hopefully for the better!). I really hope you get to capture some of your family's stories. They are very important to document or even just listen to. Even if you just do it bit by bit and you can't do it alone! In my mind, sometimes the best recorder is your own body. I would like to think that we can listen deeply to our ancestors/family stories and pass them down by word of mouth or at least express them in some way with our bodies. Sadly that's becoming more of a challenge, hey. I am very much supportive of documentation.

When I made my short radio story "27," my grandpa visited me then...sending me some kind of message to keep making radio. I have been feeling defeated by my office job lately... I always told myself I'd only stay there for one year but lately it's been tough to be there and then switch to doing what I really love—working with sound and radio. I'm working it out...crying a lot too.

I think right now in the world with social media as you described perfectly—"the glow up"—and with the political climate, there is a lot of verbal vomit. I support people telling their stories and bringing balance to what is unjust, but at the same time I really crave quietness and non-verbal ways of expressing ourselves. I also really crave sustainable systems of care. It's okay to not know the answer and it's okay to not be able to access ourselves sometimes.

+++

Thursday 18 October 10.08PM (AEST)

Hi Jeannine,

I was reading back on our conversation, which has been so nourishing for me, and I am thinking about the labour of listening and complex feelings around "doing what you love."

Today I was recording two hours worth of interviews for a freelance podcast job I'm doing. By the end I was exhausted. I couldn't really work out why until I got home later today and just felt tired and needy. I craved someone to care for me and the first thing I thought of was my need for a lover to do that for me (I'm not currently dating anyone, but the thought came to mind). After crying I realised that I do a lot of support work for others and listening is part of that. When I'm recording interviews it requires me to "tune in" and listen. In the projects that

are close to my heart I immerse myself completely and sometimes I find myself exhausted later on. I wonder if this process is necessary to doing what I love. Is it my frame of mind? Or do I need to work out better boundaries with my practice?

Sometimes I think my deep romantic relationships are not that different from the projects that are close to my heart—a mix of struggle and intense bliss.

+++

Saturday October 20, 2018 8:17 PM PST

Hi Hằng,

Lessons I've gleaned from the mistakes I've made during oral history gathering: I am responsible for after care and it isn't humane or sustainable to just extract stories without follow up, relationship building, and some kind of reciprocity. I need to apply this among ourselves too. How do we create sustainable systems of care? What would you find most beneficial and supportive to you in an ideal sustainable system of care? How do we ask for this and model this in our own lives?

You really struck me with this: "sometimes the best recorder is your own body." How does your body record, capture, channel or manifest things: stories, ancestors, happiness, happenings, etc? Despite popular belief, I like to move my large body. I like to sweat and move and dance and be active. I used to like to dance (badly) alone in my apartment to disco and salsa or cumbia music. I haven't moved my body in a long time. I haven't been to the gym in a long time or out in public so much (again, that kind of agoraphobia and embarrassment forming). Today, I thought of you and your words as I danced to one of my favorite tracks, "Enjoy Your Life," by Oby Onyioha. I don't own the record but I find her to be so beautiful and stylish here:

Reading your words made me happy even if the words or subject matter itself weren't wholly cheerful. I thought I should dance that out in some way so I did.

Yes, I do think that these feelings/thoughts about ancestors have come up for a reason. I'm aging, they're aging. Now that I haven't been a student for quite some time and I've matured a bit, I see how finite time is. I notice how long I've been away. I notice how I don't know my family. I notice how many events and important happenings I should have been present at. I notice how little I see my grandmothers and how smart, precious, integral, strong they are. I am left in awe when I think how I am related to these brilliant matriarchs. I take it for granted. Also, I feel especially vulnerable. I am kind of out in the world trying to make and ascribe meaning to myself and do something worthwhile. Because I am so uncertain and because I haven't created a clear destination for myself, I long for their wisdom, love and energy.

I find we're so wrapped up in being perceived as useful, productive, successful (by whose metric, anyway?) or hardworking in order to feel valuable or worthwhile. I think that it is a big deal that you're honest with yourself about your feelings of defeat around your job. There is such shame around not having it all figured out or if we aren't satisfied with the job we're in. We're deemed as completely "ungrateful" or told that we're doing life wrong. Listen to yourself. You are right. It is ok to feel this way. You feel this way for a reason. You deserve to create a reality for yourself wherein you do as much of what you love as possible AND make a living. I know it is far easier said than done.

Office/corporate environments are so unnatural, unsettling and draining. I get certain people thrive in them or at least learn how to cope and make it work in their favor. I truly have trouble with it. I have trouble with the sitting all day and the non-stop computer work, the quick turnaround time for tasks and projects, demands that don't have much meaning for me. It is ok to want more for ourselves. It is ok to feel disconnected and dissatisfied and off-track. We aren't failures for it. We aren't hopeless for it. We're allowed to realize our method of paying the bills is just that for now. We can demand more and believe in ourselves, I think. But this is hard…and what if it never comes? Some days are better than others.

I am happy you're crying a lot, especially if it's restorative and expelling. There is such an energy behind crying and letting the water flow out of you. I hope it feels good. If not, that's cool too.

I admire that you were blunt about the fact that you wanted a romantic partner to be there for you and to reciprocate the labor you put in elsewhere. Romantic love, attention, affection, being cared for romantically is a necessity for a lot of us even though it isn't treated as such. We're constantly told to restore ourselves or look within or solely rely on ourselves. This is all well and good and necessary. But it denies us what we need and it denies us from receiving too. We become convinced we shouldn't ask for these things from romantic partners. Maybe we shouldn't. Maybe we can never glean this from romantic relationships. I've never thought about that.

You ask such important questions about doing what you love. Boundaries seem easiest to erect in situations that are black and white not so much when it is murkier. For instance, like when it has to do with work we love. Popular discourse around following your passion or whatever, is extremely classist, sexist and ableist. Certain kinds of people are afforded this luxury with ease. Certain kinds of people are given the freedom and respect to do so full time. Doing what you love doesn't look a certain way. It can't look the same for everyone, can it? I think you're right in asking if a certain kind of love is required to "do what you love." Often people who embark on their own passion projects or enterprises state that they had some kind of obsession with their goal. The workaholism and dysfunction that emerges around achieving their obsession is scary, quite frankly. Is that feasible and sustainable for everyone? Is this possible alone? I'd argue no. I'd argue it's somewhat of a ruse. If it's not a ruse, the models out there, again seem to be highly exploitative or dysfunctional. Maybe the kind of love required to "do what you love" is more nuanced. Can it not be obsessive and manic? Why does that get romanticized? Maybe it's a tempered love that is more tied to a greater love of self and a desire to tend to ourselves. A kind of love that doesn't engulf and become rabid or self-exploitative in its pursuits? A love that doesn't expire or that doesn't need to be proven by how many angel investors, hours, awards, or how much debt we go into to make dreams happen? Can you imagine a kind of love applied to your work like that?

Davey Davis

+

Andrea Abi-Karam

I've long been drawn to the epistolary exchange between writers. Before I was involved in any sort of creative community, I turned to these exchanges with an urgent desire to know what it was like to be a part of a network of people thinking, writing, & fucking. The unarchived moments of what precedes the published book, the historic performance, what were they thinking about & what were they wearing. I need time to think through things, to peel back layers to reach the various points of obsession that drive my writing. This epistolary exchange provides little snapshots of thought spirals between Davey Davis [SF Bay Area] & myself [Brooklyn] over about a week's time. We set out to correspond every day for seven days, back and forth, and as often happens when we impose forms on ourselves, we break them.—AAK

<u>Day 1</u>

9/24: 2:48PM EST, Andrea

I spent the morning promoting the reading I'm doing tonight with Lauren Levin & Oki Sogumi—two friends & comrades I met in Oakland—& reading Discipline Press's latest achievement, S*exiness: Rituals, Revisions & Reconstructions*, edited by Tamara Stantibañez that I picked up at the New York Art Book Fair this last weekend. Since moving to New York, I've been thinking about all of my networked-connections (in the cyborg/affinity sense, not the give me a job sense). I met Oki in 2012 & Lauren in 2014. All of these connections forged through poetry, riot & a proximity bound by politics & the desire to make an attempt at imagining a better world. I'm also thinking of how you & I existed in proximity for several years without ever fully meeting until the six month mark before I moved away & am grateful for the epistolary form that houses intimate ties across distance & time. I carry these ties around with me everywhere, the same way I carry a book around inside myself, right below my sternum until it becomes something, & then, begin again.

+++

9/24 1:33 pm PST, Davey

I know Oki! We got to know each other during Occupy at UC Davis. I hadn't seen her in years, but she came to a reading I did for my book at Wooden Shoe in Philly last winter and we caught up. She's lovely, and so is her work.

"Networking" always reminds me of *Network* (1976), which reminds me of *Christine* (2016), both of which are films about people overwhelmed by modernity killing themselves on live TV (*Christine* is actually based on a true story). It makes me think about the double-edged sword of social media and the redefining of proximity/connection by digital spaces. When it creates community or whatever, particularly among radical & leftist & queer people, it feels good, and when it makes you feel like a bug under a microscope—but, like, a bug compelled to fulfill a content quota with actual, tangible deterrents for failing to participate—that does not feel good, not even when you get that hit of dopamine for playing into their hands or algorithms or whatever. There's this insidious aspect of late capi-

talism that makes the carrying of those ties burdensome, sometimes. Making art feels like an antidote to that.

I wish we had gotten to know each other sooner, but at least we're having that long-distance experience so we know it's real.

I don't know if the books live inside me, but where else would they be?

Day 2

9/25 6:26 PM EST, Andrea

Glitch glitch glitch. The reading was so good! Oki & Lauren were of course both amazing, great crowd, like an eager to listen crowd, wow. A new friend and au-thor I work with at Nightboat was there and today sent me this incredible blurb/review of my performance:

> "Thanks for the total energy and provocation of your reading last night. You model what a desired community formation looks like--no beating around the bush: direct demand, direct depiction. A performance of power as collective, queer, feral, trans, polyphonous cry, urging forth a sociality of togetherness that refuses hate and other toxic modalities. Immense power and conviction. Immense grandeur. Hero-heroine sans the grandiosity of ego. This is what jus-tice looks like, i.e. can be and is, via the pathway of your words. The message rings with precision and love speaking truth to power."—Brenda Iijima

Feels really special to be reminded that performing/sharing/reading is so im-portant & to decenter the obsession with productivity/publication. I get wrapped up in the latter all too often as I'm just so immersed in it right now, working as a publicist. Writing isn't about the book product, but more about living every sec-ond as a writer. I'm constantly grappling with the concerns unwinding in my work, not only in the moments where I'm actually physically writing. In *Inferno*, Eileen Myles says something to the effect of the necessity of making yourself, the poet/writer into the object, not just the books. Was probably even more important in the past before small press proliferation. There's something here also about not being able to hide from the work, if the writing is effective, you're implicated in it, you have to be present—or it falls flat.

Anyways, some Leo stuff, my body was on the stage last night because it had to be.

+++

9/25 5:45 PM PST, Davey

This is so lovely! But it's giving me questions about you and your, like, creative identity. Is performing an essential part of being a writer for you? Would you still write if there was no aim to be published, or even read by others (I ask my-self this question a lot; the answer could be its own unread book)? You already know I hate performing—if you can call what I do performing—and maybe also that I think that fiction readings are bad/unwarranted 99% of the time. Poetry, of course, is different.

I just got out of therapy, where I'm starting to do EMDR. I am trying to un-objectify myself as well as get comfortable with the inevitable objectness of myself, as someone with a body must if they're ever going to relax. I tend not to think of books as objects anymore than I think of myself as embodying the books that I write: I think of writing more as process than production, and would like to have that same attitude toward myself as a body. Maybe when EMDR unfucks me I'll be able to tap into that feral polyphony you're working with. Probably not though. You know my sun sign.

Day 3

9/27 12:18AM EST, Andrea

Yes! That's what I'm getting at, decentering production. There's a part in *EXTRATRANSMISSION* about the question of audience/reader. I don't write with the audience in mind, but I know that there will be an audience no matter what. Maybe it's just my Leo self-importance, but I'm not concerned what they think as long as I know they'll be there? It's such a constant process. My practice of readings is multipurpose, to have a deadline to write new work, & then to test out the emotional resonance of the new work. Part of becoming visible as a poet is by doing readings; it has this whole economic lackluster thing and in turn circulates very socially. For me, it is also important to be on the stage. Or like it's important for me personally & it's important for the work. I'm trying to study models of QTPOC performance like in José Muñoz' *Disidentifications*. I want to come up with gestures not to overtake the text, but to amplify it. I've been seeing so many amazing performances in the last few months here. Feels important not to get stuck in any one genre or identity.

I just saw the final pass proofs for *EXTRATRANSMISSION*! I didn't know until today that I was going to have an acknowledgements page, so I just spent the last few hours agonizing over it. Not in a painful way, but in an excavating way. I wrote the book between 2015/2016, so I had to delve back there and connect it with the present. Also, I think I have a fever. The endless cold is truly endless. I have a four day weekend this weekend, thank god, post working the NYABF, so hopefully I can kick this cold/hellscape ailment to the curb with a healthy dose of Renee Gladman's *Prose Architectures* that I got at a deep discount at the Brooklyn Book Fest and an unsurprising relapse into *Sex & the City*. Closest I've come to EMDR is getting my collarbone tattooed after a break up. The economies of craft are so variant.

x

+++

9/27, 12:16 AM PST, Davey

"Making a poem is making an object. I always thought of them more as drawings than as texts, but drawings that are also physically enterable through the fact of language."—Anne Carson

I'm bad at writing acknowledgments. My work feels intensely personal; acknowledging others after it's finished, even if they were involved or helped me in the process, feels like making direct eye contact after being caught eating from the garbage can. I'd rather be oblique, in life and with my work: orbiting the immovable pieces, reacting to their action. I'm interested in documentary through fiction, and crafting thought and speech into something that communicates on a level beyond its components, like when pieces of gold and steel are fitted together to make a timepiece—but it still makes me feel dirty.

Day 4

9/28, 1:31 PM EST, Andrea

Ah, sorry I missed yesterday! I have two friends in town, one of whom has never been to NYC before, so we did hilarious activities like go to Central Park and Times Square. I hadn't been to either since I moved here, actually. Times Square is like fucking Blade Runner, a very influential piece of ART in my opinion. I love that quote you sent and anne carson in general. Have you read *The Glass Essay*? It's one of the best break up poems ever written in my opinion. It opens with: "I can hear little clicks inside my dream./Night drips its silver tap/down the back./ At 4am I wake. Thinking"

Also, her translation of Sappho *If Not, Winter: Fragments of Sappho*. Sappho

was the first (Western) construction of the Lyric "I" in poetry. Poetry before that was an amalgamation of the group "community" voice, like in Homer's *The Odyssey.* Sappho was the first poetic turn to the internal, "I," deep dark feelings. All poems can be deconstructed to trace this lineage of subjectivity.

Cruel Intentions heavily influenced all of my twisted ideas of romance & desire. While we walked from the subway to Central Park yesterday, we walked past the *Cruel Intentions* house on the Upper East Side. That balcony in every movie about New York. It's really fascinating to watch my friend see IRL New York and how it feels the same as movie screen New York. Simulacrum abound.

9/30, 12:22am PST, Davey

I have read *The Glass Essay,* but only recently, I think because of Anne Boyers's Twitter? I also love Emily Brontë, and insist it is always too early for melons. I finally got around to *Eros the Bittersweet* earlier this year, which I enjoyed, but for the most part find Sappho difficult to enjoy.

I'm writing late again. Tonight, I went to the Stud to see Gayle Rubin discuss a short film she appeared in about fisting in the gay male SM subculture of San Francisco in the latter part of the twentieth century. She was wearing a necktie with a red bandana pattern—a mysterious, switchy move—and after the screening and discussion, she DJ'd. It was fabulous.

I met up with a lot of friends from the leather scene, and met a few new ones, too. I'm rarely very public as a pervert anymore; I don't go to parties, and since I almost exclusively bottom when it comes to play, I'm very selective about who gets to injure me. But I love spending time with other kinky people. The older I get, the more inextricable SM becomes from my sexuality, but at the same time, my appreciation for it as a dare-i-say-platonic activity deepens. This kind of sociality is very beautiful and mystical and fulfilling to me, I'm sorry to report, which is perhaps why I'm intrigued by Rubin's account of a fisting scene that was, in some respects, desexualized—in part because decontextualized from heteronormativity, and in part because it centered the anus and the fist, rather than the "genitalia," as Rubin put it. It was sexual, but more/less than sexual, more about an intense, embodied experience (one that was less strictly homosexual than you'd think) than fucking per se, though of course you can't have fist fuckers without, you know, fucking. It's a pleasurable paradox.

Day 5

10:37PM EST, Andrea

Ah, the STUD, yes! Your night sounds amazing. I need to come back and go to the STUD before it moves locales on New Year's. I went back to the Whitney today with some friends to see the last day of the David Wojnarowicz show. I thought it would be more crowded than it was. I sat in the film room for a long time and sat on the floor, back leaning against the wall, tiny gridded notebook on the firm cushions just writing. I generally don't love traditional ekphrastic writing, but I did it for the "Covered in Time & History: The Films of Ana Mendieta" at BAMPFA last year & I did it for this. Film is what sets it off for me. It's not a genre I'm well-versed in, but opens up something to enter into an outpour. I'm so glad I had the chance to return to it. I wanted to write the first time I went to it, but I was on a first date with someone and I needed not to be watched. There's such a fine, brutal line between visibility and surveillance. The exhibit made me feel profoundly sad & very turned on. Part of what I wrote was about getting fucked nonstop for 8 hours by late stage capitalism. Horror-desire. Maybe that's what queerness is. I hated all the Whitney copy about the exhibit, felt so erasing of queer community and the vastness of the AIDS crisis, how it was individualized on DW. David would have hated it. I hate the way gay icons become co-opted after death, after they literally can't fight anymore.

On the walk from the Whitney to a diner, we walked to the end of Christopher Street to look at the ruins of gay cruising. It's fall here & the air a little crisp. There were straight people laying around on the new Hudson River pier. We looked fabulous in the sun at the edge of dusk.

I also went to the NYU Bobst Library as they had a companion exhibit to the Whitney show, lots of process/visual/performance/painting notes & sketches for DW's pieces, which was so cool to see. I took some pix & attached them for you! It'll be up through October, but not sure if you'll get a chance to see. I was with one of my friends who went to NYU and she took us to the bathroom on the fourth floor where she used to hook up. And also accidentally set off the fire alarm for a sec trying to check out the stairwell.

10/1 3:23 PM PST, Davey

I had a similar reaction when I was at the Whitney a few weeks ago. There's a vivid memory of the room where you hear the recording of his voice. I stood there for awhile listening, looking out over the docks, the water. It was hot outside, and very bright.

I only began exploring Wojnarowicz late last year (I was delighted when my friend, Charlotte Shane, sent me a copy of *The Weight of the Earth* this summer when I was healing from surgery), but the image of him with his mouth sewn shut feels as though it has been living inside me for a very long time. There is something about his pleasure-seeking that is remarkable to me. It's not escapist (trauma-tized) but actualized, probing; that kind of curiosity is a rare quality, I think. It's actual pleasure-seeking rather than numbness-seeking. When you're reading or listening or looking at/to him, his reaction to the world seems like the most natural thing in the world, but then I look around and see how very few people (that I know, anyway) are able to do that, not through any fault of their own, but because that horror is so all-consuming.

SPACE MOUNTAIN®
Disneyland.

GHOST GALAXY

2018

© DISNEY

Emerson Whitney

+

Claire Boyle

Over the last few weeks, writer Emerson Whitney and I exchanged long, rambling, sometimes mundane, often embarrassing, always treasured voice memo confessions—usually recorded lying in bed with the lights off. Amongst the confessions, which we sent on a vaguely nightly basis, we also discussed Emerson's exquisite memoir Heaven, coming out from McSweeney's in 2020. We spoke about the act of memoir, about what it means to confess, about transness, and genre, and family, and canine euthanasia, and flaming chili peppers on ratemyprofessor.com. Before this correspondence began, we'd spoken exactly twice on the phone, once chaperoned by Emerson's agent before finalizing the book deal, and once more to discuss their updated first chapter. The following has been edited for readability and length, as the full correspondence sprawled over fifteen thousand words and we'll spare you that.

Sun, Sep 30, 6:23 PM, Claire
Hey Emerson, it's Claire! I'm sitting here in my living room. I just got back from Disneyland for my future sister-in-law's bachelorette party. We spent fifteen and a half hours in Disneyland yesterday. I didn't know that the park was open for that long in one single day, but it is. We got there at 8 am and I promptly got a flask confiscated from me from security, with a bunch of eight year olds and their parents watching. It was horrifying. But I'm excited to start this correspondence. To kick it off, I thought I'd ask about reentering something you've been working on for years, your forthcoming memoir *Heaven*. What about reentering this book are you excited about, and what are you hesitant about?

Sun, Sep 30, 6:37 PM, Claire (again)
Okay, I know I just sent you a voice memo but I had another idea that could be fun: at the end of every day sending each other confessional voice memos about things we did that day that we…shouldn't have. Thoughts?

Sun, Sep 30, 10:01 PM, Emerson
Hey Claire. Oh my god, this is awesome. Your Disneyland story sounds awful, but I love this idea of the confessional. I'm trying to think of today…I…said the F word to a young child, after he threw a metal truck at my knee. I didn't want to say it but it hurt. And I said it. So…that was me today! I hope you're doing great.

I'm really excited about the process of *Heaven*—I'm super excited about working with you. The magic that happens when there're many hands in something like this is really exciting to me. And I guess what makes me nervous is, I come from a line, of femmes actually, who are so serious about writing the scariest thing possible, and I think of Cixous and Anzaldúa and Maggie [Nelson]. And Maggie and Cixous were basically like, "Write the scariest book you possibly could," and so I did. And that means I do have to confront the enormity of releasing that onto the world, as kind of the bright crows of my worst fear. But I think they're beautiful crows, or whatever, I tried to make it really beautiful. And, I don't know, scary things can be beautiful.

Sun, Sep 30, 10:04 PM, Emerson (again)

Oh hey, it's me again. I'm making you a second one, too, because I realized that this is also an experiment in listening comprehension. For whatever reason, I didn't re-listen to yours in response. So actually I could be wrong about the question you asked me. But it's kind of interesting to only listen once? Also, I just sent it to you totally unedited, so I don't know, maybe those are things we do? You tell me!

Sun, Sep 30, 11:14 PM, Claire

Hey Emerson! I love the idea of only being able to listen once, and to not edit them. With those two rules in mind, I'm going to give you my first confessional, which is that I rerecorded those voice memos…more than once. You got, like, take three on both of them. Which is very embarrassing to admit.

Sun, Sep 30, 11:15 PM, Claire (again)

I've just been told that re-listening to your voice memos counts as editing even if you don't rerecord it. What do you think?

Mon, Oct 1, 10:35 PM, Emerson

Hey Claire, what's up? Here's my voicemail for you tonight. And, in response to your question from yesterday—my gut says maybe but my head says no, because sometimes it's nice just to hear our own voices. And I think we get to have that. You know? So, the confession I have for you today is that I spent most of the day worried about whether or not my students like me, and that is the truth. I don't know if they liked a recent reading, and I spent a lot of time thinking about that. And whether or not I'm cool. In their minds. I used to be really proud of the flaming chili pepper on ratemyteacher.com from a while ago. And, also really proud of the fact that on ratemyteacher.com, nobody knows my pronouns, which is hysterical in that format because the entries somehow alternate pronouns one after the other. Which I now find completely amusing. But I don't…I don't know if they like me. And they might not. One of them might not! I look forward to confessing something else tomorrow. I hope you're doing great.

Mon, Oct 1, 10:53 PM, Claire
Hey Emerson! I would covet a chili pepper, too, on Rate My Professor. You mentioned coming from a line of femmes who are proponents of writing the scariest thing, and I wanted to ask if them being femme is related to that instinct to write the scariest thing, or if that was anecdotal. Oh, and I had another question! You mentioned that your students didn't know your pronouns on Rate My Professor, which is as good a time as any to ask, what are your pronouns? Mine are she/her.

My confession is that I was talking to my mother on the phone today, and I talked about myself the whole time and didn't ask her anything. She just got finished teaching a Qi Gong class and I didn't even ask her how the class went. She has this rule now with her mother. My grandma talks about herself a lot, and my mom's one rule is that she has to ask my mom one question, and then can talk about herself for the rest of the time. Which is so small, and I don't know, I feel bad being another person that's doing that for her.

Tue, Oct 2, 11:10 PM, Emerson
Hey Claire! How's it going. This one's kind of later than I've done before, but I loved your questions, and I super hear you about not asking about somebody else. So, I was thinking about your question regarding if the femme thing was anecdotal or if it was relevant to the scariest thing. I think this is really interesting for us to talk about in the realm of doing this confession project. I guess I was just giving a nod to the gender of the writing lineage that I ascribe to, or a gender in a pantheon of genders that I ascribe to. But I think it is interesting to talk about the scariest thing as it bumps against what is often considered confessional writing. I know some folks that were on book tour at the same time, and their autobiographical books might be considered by some as confessional literature. They're both cis women, and one of the folks is a white woman and the other is woman of color, and they were both super frustrated about that narrative around their work. They were like, "Well, you didn't ask the cis, straight, white guy if his autobiography was confessional," which I think, if I'm reading this discourse of theirs right, is that it was kind of about how quote unquote women's writing that doesn't come from cis white men is often considered therapeutic, and not literary. Which could be considered a devaluing of the enormous work that it takes to craft a project, and all the hands that go into it, and all of the time and the care and consideration for the language.

I also do think it's interesting for our project to be like, well, what does it mean to confess? What even is the etymology of it? I have so many students that ask, "Why is it not just terrible and masturbatory to be writing about ourselves?" As someone who belongs to a variety of marginalized groups, it does feel like, of course it's important for us to write about ourselves. But as a person who also belongs to a handful of dominant groups, I question what it means to write about myself. Where can I leave gaps in my work for other people? And if I use my subjective "I" as I want to use it, which is to allow it to be a portal for other readers to insert their own "I," how is it then that I confess? I don't know. I always have an audience back here in my mind, I have the hardest core trans folk, my trans femme people that I care about so much, particularly Black trans femmes, and femmes of color, that are like, "We're just fighting for our lives out here." Those folk have trained me to think. I always have that discourse at the forefront of my mind, which is like, how is anything else important when my sisters are dying? So, that's my first bit. I'm sure you asked more stuff that I forgot—oh, my pronouns! He or they. They is good, he's good; those are good right now.

But what do I have to confess? At one of my jobs they asked all of the faculty of color to participate in an oral history of their participation in the college and whether or not the institution was racist. So this person, who is a former teacher, and is a friend and colleague of mine, asked me to participate. And I was like, "Wait, why? I don't experience racism, I don't experience colorism. I certainly show up in the world as white." But he knows about my family, and knows about my history with my grandmother. He was like, "You should do this because you get this special perspective because you show up in the world as white. You get to hear a lot of racist stuff that goes on." And he's right, I do. But my confession is that I feel super conflicted about ever participating in any way like this. My aim is to always show up for racial justice.

You may have noticed in the book—there's a time when I thought my grandmother may have been Hawaiian when I was a little kid. And I talk about my boobs and how some of these dudes I used to hook up with when I was younger would be like, "Oh your Nat Geo boobs," because I had these big, brown areolas and they thought they were, like, "ethnic," they'd say, which was really creepy. But when I cut off my boobs—which had always been identified with my grandma because my mom would always point that out that I had inherited her chest—did I cut off my connection to that part of myself? So I was raised with this splat of racism that happened toward my grandmother. She would really hate that I was making an issue of it. Because she definitely operates in the world as an honorary white person, or wants to, even though racist stuff happens to her. I think it's important to be in the mess of it, and the discomfort. As someone who doesn't deal with colorism on a day-to-day basis, this is an important place of discomfort for me to inhabit. The fact that she would be pissed weighs on me a lot. But it's true, that's what it is. There we are. That's what I think. Yeah, I hope you're great

Thu, Oct 4, 1:00 AM, Claire
Hey Emerson, I'm sorry to send this so late. I'm sitting in my childhood kitchen right now. I just got off the plane in Chicago for an audio festival, and I'm sitting and eating tuna fish off crackers, which is the first thing I do whenever I come home. I've been thinking so much about what you said, particularly about the tendency for female autobiographical writers to be thought of as writing confessional, and how that connects to this thing we're doing. You've found the link between these two threads of conversations! Which is a very satisfying moment. It got me thinking if we should, so as not to play into that history, call it something other than a confessional. The only thing I could think of is that it's not confessing, it's—oh my god I already forget what it was! It's revealing. It's corny, but maybe it's something to work from. My confession—no no no! I already messed it up!—my reveal is that when I got home, I got in bed with my mom to say hi, and immediately farted all the plane farts I had been holding in right in her bed. And I have a question I wanted to ask in the spirit of confessionals, and autobiographical work, and *Heaven* specifically. Who, if anyone, are you most nervous of reading this book when it comes out? Is there any moment that reveals something that you had never told a person?

Thu, Oct 4, 6:35 PM, Emerson
Hey Claire, what's up. Oh my god, this is good stuff. It turns out we're both on the road. I'm driving on the five, going to the Bay today. There's a part right by these cows where the smell is so bad that I noticed one time I was unconsciously trying to turn the stereo volume up in my car, as a way to drown out the smell, which…doesn't work. I saved your stuff to listen to until I was almost there. I want to tell you that I googled the etymology of confession, and it's

actually fucking awesome. *Con* is "with," and the *fession* is "to admit." But then if you keep digging, the etymology of admit is "to let in." Duh, but it's so good, actually, to think that we're letting in. I'm so into that. How cool is it that the confession is actually like an invitation? That's fucking cool. It's like an invitation for other people, or a reader, to access their own experience. I love that concept. I think we've sufficiently unpacked it to the point that now I have jubilation.

So, alright, as for my current confession. Here's something that links to this idea of letting in. Yesterday in my class we were reading Eli Clare's book, *Exile and Pride*, which is from 1999. Some of the social justice language is a little outdated, but he's still writing at the intersection of transness and disability and also some environmental activism, which is cool. But I could tell the class's energy around it was flagging a bit because of the ways Eli was presenting things. So I told them a story that I don't even think I've told anyone, but I did write about it in *Heaven*. I was given that book when I was twenty, in undergrad, and I had been saying the R word a lot. Like, I liked the sound of it in my mouth, because it sounded very New York to me. I had just moved in with my uncle after high school and I wanted to have a New Yorker attitude and use my words to emphasize my New York attitude and I thought that was part of what I embraced about that word. But also, when I was questioned, I would say, "Well, I was in special ed forever and I had that word used against me all the time, so I'm reclaiming it." But this person who was also trans came up to me and was like, "Hey, can I talk to you for a minute? When you said that word it really hurts my feelings and I would love it if you would read this book *Exile and Pride*." I realized in reading the book and talking to that person that my desire for reclamation was totally thin compared to my desire to show up for this person with compassion and attention and care. I told that story to my students, and I could tell they immediately connected differently to the book, and to me, and they started telling their own stories like that. Because we all have blind spots. I'm embarrassed by that story, and so it was kind of a confession. It did invite them in, and I could tell the energy completely changed. It was cool, and that was when I looked up the etymology, because I was like, oh my god, I just did that! Maybe it's because of this project with Claire that I'm feeling very free.

Thu, Oct 4, 6:37 PM, Emerson (again)
Hey my friend. So I just realized that I've been talking away for a while and the

memo had stopped recording at some point. I was going to answer the question about who I'm scared to read this book. Definitely my mom. My mentor recommended that I tell her about it, and that it's on its way into the world. I didn't want to at all. But my mentor was like, "You don't want to surprise her. Surprising people with this kind of stuff is harder." I texted my mom. Which is the form of communication we're using right now. I've not actually spoken to her in quite a while. I'm not sure why she doesn't want to talk to me, but she doesn't want to talk to me. Which is totally okay, that's where she's at. I was on this random little island where she lives this summer, and she didn't want to see me there. Which was sad because I passed her house three or four times in the car. She's not down for communicating with me right now in any other way than text but I'll take it. It's very 2018 of her. Anyway, I texted her and it was actually really awesome because I never tell her about things that I do. She doesn't know that I graduated from a PhD program. She really thinks that if your hands are bleeding than you've done a really good job at work, and if they're not bleeding then you should probably reevaluate what you do with your life. Sometimes it does feel like I'm stepping over her body to get to some of these accomplishments, and I don't want it to be like that. So I think this gesture of being honest with her was really important because it does let her in in a way that she deserves to be let in. I think I have a lot of survivor's guilt in some ways. Sometimes I wonder if I'm where I'm at today because my mom taught me with all her actions what I don't want to do, and in a way it feels like an enormous sacrifice that she made. So when I texted her I said, "Hey mom, I wrote this book and a lot of it is about our relationship, and I just wanted to give you the opportunity to look at it before it comes out if you want. I also want to tell you that it is kind of a thank you note to you for teaching me how to read and write and how to appreciate doing that, and I love you." And she wrote back, and she's never so effusive so it was kind of shocking and I got really emotional, actually. But she was like, "Em, everybody knows our life has been no picnic. Write whatever you want, I'm not worried about it. Bravo, I love you." And she sent me a bunch of red hearts, and like a GIF of a bear. It was so kind and I am just really grateful that that was her response.

But I'm scared of her reading the more contemporary parts of the book where I was feeling uncomfortable around what I call in the book her titanic childishness. Which in a lot of ways I admire about her. When she's in a good place she's so ebullient and bouncy. She speaks in this language that she invented. In the house I can deal with it but in public I get super uncomfortable and embarrassed. Five years ago we went to the AT&T store and she walked up to the guy at the counter and she was talking baby talk to him. And I was like, "Oh my god, mom, please." It's not just baby talk—she also has these other words. For example, *gingcuttie* is her word for lizard. And *papaonderhleesh* is a dog on the leash. Whenever that leaks out into what I would consider her real life, I'm totally embarrassed. I don't one hundred percent know why. I guess I just…I guess in relation to what I'm writing about so much in *Heaven*, I guess I wonder what that means about me. And in reality, it doesn't need to say anything about me. It's really just where she's at in life, and that's beautiful. If she feels good when she'd doing that, hell yeah.

I guess in general, I'm always aware that when I ask my insides how much of my childhood made me up and how much of this is innate, there's not really ever an answer. I'm nervous about how people will take that. In the book I say that Karen Barad, this queer physicist based out of U.C. Santa Cruz, said to me, "Straight people aren't wondering what caused their straightness." So the fact that I sit around wondering if my experience of womanness, through my mom, has anything to do with my gender and sexuality as it exists today. Of course, it is all part of living in a white-supremacist cis-hetero-patriarchy, but my mom too? I mean that's why I'm embarrassed about my mom at the AT&T store, because I'm like, "Is someone going to look at my mom, and then look at me and be like, of course that person is this way! Because of this woman." And I also don't know why that's so troubling if it's true. I guess because I would like more agency than that, or some kind of innate truth.

Fri, Oct 5, 11:46 PM, Claire
Hey Emerson, guess who? I'm lying in bed and so exhausted. I'm glad that you reached out to your mom, and I'm glad to hear that that's how she responded. My confession…I should just let it go. Maybe I'll just tell it to you, and in telling it to you I will be letting it go. Which is maybe the point of this whole thing, right? But I'm at this conference on an ill-advised press pass—I'm not a journalist by any regard. But I've always wanted to go to this festival, so I said, "Sure, why not?" and went with the idea that I would write about interdisciplinary audio work, because I'm interested in doing that kind of work right now. So I think that was my first mistake, this ulterior motive. And the second mistake is that I thought I'd wing it. And I talked to a producer today and—I mean, she was

lovely, and a lot of it I really enjoyed. But there was a certain point where I kept trying to jam my idea—I'm sorry I sound verklempt, I'm having such intense acid reflux, I'm having acid travel back up my esophagus right now and burn my mouth as I'm talking—but anyway, long story short I was just trying to jam this really vague, undeveloped, poorly-intended story into this interview. On top of that is the fact that these people are radio journalists who are so familiar with interviewing and getting a story from a person, which made me doubly nervous about being judged by my subject as I was interviewing them. But it's alright! Tomorrow's another day! Oh, I know exactly that spot on the five that you're talking about. My final confession is that I kind of like the smell…it's really intense, so intense, and I don't like it for very long, but I like it a little bit. Thanks as always, I immensely look forward to getting to listen to your blurps. I got an email today from Wolfman, checking in, and I think we should make the 9th our last day. So let's see, what day is it today, oh man, I think it's the 5th…

Fri, Oct 5, 11:47 PM, Claire (again)
As fate would have it, my recording also cut itself off, and I went on yammering. The conclusion was let's take it to the ninth and see how that goes.

Sat, Oct 6, 10:27 PM, Emerson
Hey Claire, what's up. I'm back in LA. I'm sitting at my desk which is actually a gigantic table. I wanted a gigantic table as a desk, which I didn't totally think through. But it means my entire apartment is a desk. I'm into it, actually. But, not everybody else is, I think. It's sort of funny when they walk in because I have tons of books on the floor, and a giant table desk. It kind of makes me look like I'm Vincent Price or something. My confession is that I've been trying to stay off Facebook, and today I noticed when it got quiet that I was spelling the typing in my head of Facebook. In my mind I was going F-A-C-E. I was typing it into the search box in my mind. Obviously today has been a chill day for me, uh, cuz that's what I got. I hope you're going great! I'm sorry to hear about all the difficulty at that conference. It sounds tiring. But it also sounds cool! Going to the ninth sounds good! Let's do it!

Sat, Oct 6, 11:32 PM, Claire
Hey Emerson. I made it through! Today was so good. So much better than

yesterday. Back on track! Back on top! I was thinking a lot about *Heaven* today. Specifically in two moments—I was talking to this multi-media artist, Alison Kobayashi, who does this incredible piece called "Say Something Bunny." It was one of the most inspiring artist talks I've seen in a long time. Her piece is rooted in this found 50s-era audio recording of this family at a dinner party who's testing out this new recording device they got. She studied this recording for years and learned all she could learn about this family, and extrapolated and imagined, and brought this night to life. She was talking about this feeling of getting to know the story from this tape, and then eventually meeting one of the youngest sons from it after the fact. And it made me think a lot about reading *Heaven* and that feeling of talking to you for the first time after spending so much time with your text.

And then I was talking to a friend of mine about femme writers writing memoirs being received as confessional. And she said that when she thinks of memoir she thinks of it being a very feminine genre. And one, I wondered if I believed that to be true. And I wondered if it had to do with emotional intelligence and with the tendency generally for women to be more comfortable investigating their experiences and relationships, in a way that in my experience I haven't seen quite so developed in the men in my life.

My confession is that I took the train into the city for this conference and I didn't pay for it. I became an expert of this in high school. You just look the other way when the conductor is walking by, and you put your headphones on, or you close your eyes and look like you're sleeping. And when the conductor came by, I felt this surge of anxiety like I felt when I was in high school. And then I thought, oh, I'm an adult. I'll just pay for this ticket because that's what adults do. They don't steal a six-dollar train ride. But then he came closer to me and my instincts just kicked in. And it worked! I felt a little guilty about it, but I'm six dollars richer today, so, what're you gonna do?

Sun, Oct 7, 10:33 PM, Emerson
Claire what's up, it's Emerson. I hope you're doing great. It was so good to get your message, I always love to hear what's going on. I loved that you thought about *Heaven* today. Thank you for that. I'm still totally honored that you think about it, that it lives in you. Once, Maggie [Nelson] told me she was struck by that line where I talk about overalls on my little-kid self and I mention the snap

catching against my nipples. She pulled me aside at one point and was like, "I cannot get that image out of my head." There are several images that she could pull out at the ready after reading it a while earlier, and I was so struck by that. I'm having the same experience hearing you interact with it, because it does feel like it belongs to you and everyone else in that way, and those images are now our images. It's amazing to let my hands off the dove of that. Watching it leaving my sightline every day is really a cool feeling.

What else was I going to tell you—oh yeah! Your friend had suggested that their experience of memoirists were mostly femme people, or cis-women, I'm assuming. I guess I would refute that. If we were talking about the *My Struggle* series which has had so much fame, the Karl Ove series—I don't think there's anything more indulgent than writing six books about one's self called *My Struggle*. And there are many many many more examples like that that I could bring up. The stereotypical recovery memoir is often considered to be a cis-male project. And I don't know if I have this flipped, which I may, but I'm a huge believer in the act of autobiography versus memoir, because memoir in my mind means one shot. You write one story about yourself and then you're done. But I'm really deeply invested in the practice of autobiography, which is life-writing. So I can write an autobiography about this storm chasing that I did last summer that I'm working on right now, I can write an autobiography about the experience of my childhood, and I can also write, as Maggie Nelson did, to bring her back, about falling in love with the color blue. So, when we think about autobiographical writing being that vast, then it usually reduces that trope. Because it's just not accurate, in my mind. I think maybe Cixous would like the idea that women have more access to an emotional intelligence, like her *ecriiuré féminin* or whatever, but there are so many trans people who have come and been like, "Hey, hello, that is an essentialist idea." That any gender has an essential knowing that any other gender doesn't is an attempt to make something biological, or physiological, that isn't, or make something inherent that isn't. So that kind of line of inquiry is interesting, too. As a trans person I do spend a lot of time also trying to refute the perception of any kind of inherent hybridity in my work that might be aligned with being trans. Sometimes there's a suggestion that my work is experimental and hybrid, and trans people write like that. And there's also sometimes the suggestion that trans is inherently a radical identity. And I would argue that it's not, necessarily. Maybe non-binary identity is, I don't know. But I don't necessarily think that there's an inherent quality to any of these things in an essential way. I'm just thinking these things through like everyone else.

Okay, confession for the day…my six-year-old buddy told his parents right when I got there today that I was swatting him with a fly swatter the last time I was hanging out. They were laughing about it but I was still like, "Oh no! That sounds bad." But we were! We totally were! It was part of a game where he was a fly, and he wanted to play like that, and he was also swatting me. At this age he's learning how to triangulate. Tonight when I said, "Hey buddy, no more TV," he said, "Mamma's not the boss of you." He was trying to pump me up, like, you can be your own person! But I was like, "Mamma's actually super the boss, so, no." It is interesting to watch one's power ebb away in contact with a six year old who's feeling very empowered.

Sun, Oct 7, 11:59 PM, Claire
Hey Emerson, I am back in my San Francisco bedroom at long last. I am so in awe and grateful for how generous you are, and have been from the get-go, with your work and with thinking about it as this thing that has become part of the world and sharing it with me, so I just want to thank you for that generosity. And I also want to thank you for checking that essentialist line of thinking when it comes to autobiography, that was really interesting and helpful. And, my confession. My confession is my childhood dog is dying right now. He's been having these seizures, and he's got Cushing's disease that makes his back sway and his stomach jut out, and has been wiping out when he turns corners too quickly and if it wasn't so sad it would be a little funny. But it's just so pathetic. He's just stopped engaging on all levels except for pure survival—there's absolutely no joy left in him, or pleasure. The vet suggested that she put him down, but no one else in my family will weigh in, which leaves my mom the primary burden of taking care of this dog and also the burden of deciding when to let him go. Honestly, within a day of sharing a house with this dog I was so bummed out. The sense I get is that she's ready to and wants to, but can't quite make that final leap. And this morning he was walking around the house, and my dad was feeding him sausages, so he was extra chipper, which means he was just, like, walking. And I said something without thinking like, "He's so alive! He's way too alive to kill him." Which was so the worst thing to say. I know my mom is at this place right now where she's looking for any feedback or help in making this decision and figuring out how she should be feeling about it, and it was…it was unthinking of me to have said that. I told her later that I think what-

ever she does is the right decision. But that's my confession slash regret of the day. It's good to hear from you as always. I'll talk to you soon.

Mon, Oct 8, 11:09 PM, Emerson
Hey Claire, how's it going? I'm really sorry to hear about your childhood dog and his impending passing. It's super hard. It also sounds hard to be your mom in that position. It's something I think about a lot because I'm in charge of a very small dog who loves me very much, who has a lot of special needs, as do I, so I feel very responsible for her care. I was thinking about how weird it is that pretty much at the end of everyday there's something to confess. But I can't think of anything today. Which is sort of funny—I can't even think of anything. The only thing I have to confess is that I was almost thinking about not doing this because I am so tired. But I was like, push through. Make the memo. I don't even have anything else to confess. What does that even mean? I don't know. So that's my confession for the day. I don't have one! I'll talk to you tomorrow, or soon, or, bye.

Tue, Oct 9, 12:47 PM, Claire
Hey Emerson. Today is the ninth! I don't know how that happened! I totally understand that feeling of not having a confession. I feel like it's now set off the habit in myself of digging for the confession, which won't turn off automatically. My confession for today is—you know that feeling of having clothes that you've loved for a long time and it's gotten really worn down and doesn't look how it looks in your mind's eye anymore? Which happened to me with a pair of Palladiums that I wore for years and I thought were the coolest, but you could see my socks through the toes, and they were falling apart. My friend one day looked at me and said, "Those don't look how you think they look. You need to get a new pair of shoes." I just made that realization today about the pair of underwear I'm wearing. They've been my favorite pair for years, and look absolutely ridiculous and I need to let them go. They're like see-through and full of holes, and I still see them as the sexy pair of underwear from years ago.

I don't want to forcibly try to tie things up, but I've been thinking a lot about the difference between memoir and autobiography, and the way that these genres hold a certain kind of weight or bias, and this idea that people try to ascribe a certain hybridity to the writing of trans people. And with all these things in mind

on this eve of the end of this project, I was curious how you think of *Heaven*. I think the manuscript says *Heaven: A Memoir,* and I wonder if that's how you want to see it labeled, what that means to you.

And the logistical side. I'm going to transcribe these memos and then we can go back and forth and see what we want to focus on. Because I kind of think this is going to be like fifteen pages.

And then for the sentimental part, which is just thanking you so much for being open to participating in this with me. It's been such such a treat, and I feel like it's opened a lot of things up. Thank you for being in it with me. And for sharing, and I can't wait to keep talking. Yeah, this has been so wonderful. Thanks, Emerson. I'll talk to you soon!

Tue, Oct 9, 6:29 PM, Emerson
Claire, oh my god! Wait, how is it the ninth? How did that fucking happen? I'm not ready. I just listened to your memo, and I'm just so grateful too. After I hung up my confession yesterday I was like, oh, I have one! And it was that I was like, oh, what if Claire now, after actually interfacing with me on these, is like, who is this person? Maybe I ruined whatever possibly starry idea you had of me through my work, was my fear. That's my retroactive confession from yesterday. But then I was like, no I actually think wel...'ve heard a lot of people working with their editors, and don't have that much interaction really beside comments and stuff, and I already feel way more connected to your thought process. And your generosity, too, has been amazing. When you said at the beginning that what you say is suggestions, I was sort of like, wait, really? I guess I had this impression that someone who was editing my work would come in with a red pen and then sort of peace out. So the collaborative nature of what we're doing, and the shared vision we have, is phenomenal. It's a huge gift, and I'm super pumped that you're here, virtually and in real life. So thanks, again. And thanks again for wanting to do this project, it's really fucking cool. I also agree that it's going be like fifteen pages. I actually think it's gonna be like twenty-nine pages, and if you want help with transcription let me know. And oh my god your con-fession about your underwear, I so understand. All my old underwear, because a lot of it was purple from American Apparel, is now—

Tue, Oct 9, 6:38 PM, Claire
Emerson! Your voice memo got cut off!! Unless you just really abruptly stopped talking in the middle of your sentence about American Appeal underwear. And now I'm DYING TO KNOW HOW IT ENDED. What was the end of your memo????

Barbara Browning

+

j.j. Mull

*Author, performer, and critic Barbara Browning and I don't know one another—
at least, not really. A couple of months ago, I sent her a cold e-mail introducing
myself as a "little poet" who manages a "little bookstore," and asking if she
might be interested in striking up a correspondence. She responded within a
few hours, explaining that she would be on sabbatical in Normandy for the next
few months and that she's switched all personal correspondence to the written
kind. Her "office," she explained, "is a plastic picnic table in the garden, and the
internet connection here is blissfully feeble. Although I seem to be answering
your email very quickly, that's just because it's almost noon here and you were
all I found of interest in the inbox when I opened it just now." Barbara and I
went on to send two handwritten letters simultaneously—a form of correspon-
dence that really only retroactively constitutes a conversation. We touched on
the origin of my name, Elvis Presley, Madame de Sévigné, and group psycho-
analysis, among other things. —j.j.*

Dear j.j.,

I haven't received your letter, so this one will cross it in the mail. You'd suggested such a possibility yourself, which I liked—like two people speaking to each other at the same time without being able to hear each other, but maybe later it will sound like a conversation. There are other kinds of ostensibly "failed" correspondence that I like to think about—the most extreme being the "dead letter," which I'm sure you know about. Then there's the purloined letter, which people have theorized up the wazoo, including me. And then recently I did a pretty extended exegesis of Elvis Presley's "Return to Sender." My interpretation was partly influenced by a blog post by a lawyer who pointed out some inconsistencies in the logic of the lyric. But his final piece of advice was not to pretend not to live at your legal address, even if you're pissed off at your lover, because you may stop receiving the mail you actually want.

Here's what I have from you: two brief e-mails, and a self-description—"a little poet" who manages a "little bookstore." Being a minimalist myself (at least, sort of), and on the small side, both of these terms appealed to me. I didn't want to over-research you (I'm an academic with a bad habit of going down rabbit holes), so when I googled j.j. Mull, I only opened one page, which was an Urdu-English dictionary. The English word "Mull" was preceded by some Urdu script which was apparently interpreted by Google as "jJ." Although I managed not to over-research you, I did over-research Urdu, and it looks to me like the script above "Mull" ends in <u>zhain</u> <u>gaf</u>. "Mull" in this dictionary is defined as, "Thin plain muslin, meddle, mess," or, alternatively, "Make win [sic] into a hot drink," which should obviously read "Make wine into a hot drink." I would have said, "Think things over," or even "Over-think things."

Well, having said I researched both Elvis Presley and Urdu Script on the internet, I guess you'll find suspect my claim that I was virtually off the internet here in Normandy, writing all my correspondence longhand and sending it in the mail. But, in fact. it's true! The internet was freaking me out a bit, what with everybody holding forth, leaping to judgement, Russian bots wreaking havoc and our idiot president ramping everything up. This summer I read the *Letters of Madame de Sévigné*, in a musty old volume I checked out of the library. I came here and made this policy of slowing down my correspondence to a snail's pace.

As I told you, my collaborator and I are here writing a book—I'm on sabbatical— and in between we're making some travels. I'd predicted it might make it hard for me to write in September as you'd proposed, and in fact we've now adjusted our schedule and are traveling soon. I'll try to respond later this month. But as I said, there's something, to me, sort of nice about a cross communication.

Warmly,

Barbara

+++

Dear Barbara,

I'm currently writing you from the Mill Valley Public Library in Marin County. It's secretly one of the nicest libraries in the Bay Area (no doubt because of its location in a removed, mega-affluent enclave, more or less inaccessible by public transit). I have access to my roommate's car this week, so I figured I'd treat myself to a little trip. All in all, it's been a very pleasant day, although I drive so infrequently, I always forget just how bad and nervous a driver I am. It wasn't a particularly long trip from Oakland, but it entailed driving across a bridge and along some small, curvy roads, all of which provoked some anxiety in me. I have a relatively nervous temperament in general. Whenever people play those con-versational games where you go around saying what kind of animal you would be, I inevitably opt for ones that are small, trembly, and nervous (i.e. bunnies, chihuahuas, mice, rodents, etc).

I guess this brings us back to my self-identification as "little" in the initial e-mail I sent you. I presented myself as a "little poet," which is typical—I'm prone to de-scribing myself in the diminutive. It's a central self-conception (smallness), that in some ways really determines how I move in and inhabit the world. You may have noticed that my handwriting is quite small. I'm also relatively small phys-ically and am the youngest of a big, working class family (I have four siblings, one of whom happens to be my twin—a whole other can of worms). The five of us kids practically lived on top of each other in a tiny three bedroom house with my parents (until they split) and my uncle Clifford. Being the youngest (in addi-tion to frail and near-sighted) always made me feel like the runt of the litter.

"j.j." (as you may or may not have guessed) is a chosen name—one which I identify with mostly on account of its smallness (two little lower case letters in a row). I mean, it's sort of a chosen name. It was originally a childhood nickname given to me by my sister as a semi-cruel, semi-playful imitation of what was, at the time, a debilitating stutter (my birth name is "Jason," thus when trying to speak my own name as a kid, it would come out as "j...j...j...," etc.). It's only been within the past year that I've fully reclaimed it as a name. In part, it feels like this way of taking back and owning the stutter—taking something that was, for the first fifteen some odd years of my life, a source of humiliation and shame, and finding a way to incorporate it, make it new. Around this time last year (September 10th, to be exact), I also suffered what ended up being a pretty severe mental break, so the adoption of "j.j." as a name felt like a way to usher in a new era. For me, it represents the onset of a renewed dedication to mental health, calm, and slowness.

Anyways, here I am, writing to you from the Mill Valley Public Library. This is probably the closest I've come to writing a "fan letter," although so far it doesn't look anything quite like that. To be totally honest, prior to a few months ago, I hadn't read all that much of your work, and only had the vaguest associations of you. On a lark, I picked up a copy of the *The Gift* and was immediately enamored with the sense of presence it facilitated—the feeling, as I think you put it, of "inappropriate intimacy." "Inappropriate," perhaps, because unexpected, or at least because it falls outside the frame of what we ordinarily conceive of as "intimacy."

Coincidentally, while reading your book I was simultaneously reading an old edition of Experiences in Groups by Wilfred Bion that someone had recently sold to the bookstore I manage. Despite it being a relatively short, fleeting moment, the fact that Bion appears briefly in *The Gift* totally delighted me. I was like, "Oh my God! She's referencing Bion!" It was honestly this little Bion moment that made me initially want to get in touch. It triggered a whole swirl of associations between your work and a set of thoughts I've been steeping in over the course of the past year.

Let me explain: so, recently I've becomes interested in (low-key obsessed with) a group psychoanalytic practice developed by Bion. "Group Relations" is the intellectual frame, broadly, with "Tavistock" being the set of methods associated with it. Maybe you're familiar? I attended my first three-day Tavistock conference in the spring and have been more or less incapable of talking or thinking about anything ever since. Each conference day lasts from 9 a.m. to 9 p.m., and is divided into what are called "here and now" events, meaning the supposed task is to remain in the emotional present tense. There are two large group sessions a day, which consist of all participants (in my experience, 45 people) sitting in a spiral formation, with three trained "consultants" scattered through-out the room. Over the course of the day, you also have several hour-long small group sessions (eight members, one consultant).

As a side note: incidentally, my small group consultant over the course of the weekend was performance scholar and artist, Andrea Fraser. I mention this not to name drop or anything, but simply as a point of interest. It's really some-thing particular about these events that you end up having these really intense, emotional experiences with a pretty wide spectrum of people. Andrea's involve-ment brings in a whole contingent of art world-adjacent folks, but there are also mental health professionals, analysts, psychology undergrads, etc. Not having much legible credibility in either academia or the art world, I had difficulty at first feeling legitimate in the eyes of the group, which, of course, was grist for the mill.

The whole frame is really different than any other therapeutic context I had been in up to that point. Seeing as the ostensible task is to remain in the "here and now," you don't generally end up revealing all that much biographical detail. By the end of the conference, I was left feeling extremely close to a group of people who, by and large, I knew almost nothing about. It produced this very particular strain of condensed intimacy. I think this is why your work resonated with my experience in Tavistock. It was on a different scale, but reading your novel left me with a similar set of feelings. I haven't fully fleshed it out for myself, but I can't help but feel that the two experiences are related in some way...that they're engaged in a similar practice. I'm not sure if that makes sense...

Sorry if this is too rambly or associative! I hope to hear from you soon, in any case, and I hope things are pleasant in France. It pleased me to hear that you're over there, given the fact that, as a younger person, I was a total francophile. I studied French literature as an undergraduate and eventually wrote my senior thesis on Proust. It feels a little embarrassing in retrospect, although I think it was all essentially an early attempt to mask my working class roots. The uncon-scious thought was something along the lines of: "What's the most bourgeois possible thing I can study?" All of that to say, I'll cop to still loving Proust.

As requested, I've included a poem, although, as it so happens, most of my writing isn't all that "little" at all. For the sake of (some) brevity, I've included whatever excerpts of a longer piece could fit onto a postcard of Frank O'Hara.

xoxo,

j.j.

Julio Linares

+

Sophia Dahlin

I met the painter Julio Linares in 2011, with the painter and tattooist Julia Garibaldi Tobias, a year after I'd moved to Oakland from Madrid. A madrileño friend had arranged for Julio and Julia, lxs Julis, to stay me while they toured California—they were going to buy a van, drive to Burning Man, and ask to be admitted. Ticketless. They won't let you in, we told them, but Julio and Julia insisted: no, we'll tell them from our hearts, we'll tell them how far we've come, show them our art—and they'll let us in.

They did not, of course. But the story is still sweet. There at the gate, Julio and Julia made friends with other idealists who'd bought the hype but not the tickets, rag-tag out of towners unaware that Burning Man is a for-profit worker-cannibalizing capitalist trashfire flickering only across the face glitter of those basking, for a few days, in the novelty of being simultaneously moneyed and dusty. They took a road trip with their new friends, and ended up living with some of them—and with me—and with other strangers—and with me again—for months before Julia left to connect with family in South America. Julio lingered, briefly got adopted by some urgent scenesters in the Mission, who threw a huge show of the portraits he made of them, and returned to Madrid.

In the time he lived here, I fell very much in love with his luminous, venomous, visionary works of art.

Julio and I did this interview over email, in Spanish (mine botched from years of disuse), all of which I've translated here. —Sophia

Sophia: For years you've painted forests, palm trees, wild animals, thick-tongued snakes. Your most recent paintings include figures that look like you, sometimes naked, sleeping, beside big cats. Are these interior landscapes? Can you find them on a map?

Julio: They are interior landscapes, basically. The truth is I'm not sure where I got this obsession...Well, yes I do, and it's very naïve and simple. When I was little, my grandfather told me stories about his characters Don Teodoro and Babalí. Babalí was the son of a tribal chief and Don Teodoro an explorer like my grandfather. They had adventures in which they shared their knowledge. My grandfather told me these stories so naturally, with so much detail, that I took for granted that I would grow up and have similar adventures. That's where my obsession began. My childish imagination, inflated by my grandfather. And this space consolidated the base from which I channel my creation. So, you can locate it in a child's fantasy.

Sophia: Wait, your grandfather was an explorer?!

Julio: My grandfather was an involuntary explorer in the Spanish Civil War, but he never went to the jungle. He made these stories up for his grandchild, living his dreams as he told them, remembering a life he didn't have, a life he would have preferred over what fell to him instead, which was the war.

Don Teodoro and Babalí come from him. I didn't realize they were fantasies until my grandfather died and I was more teenager than

120

child. But let's be clear: it didn't matter whether they were invented or experienced, I'd already taken for granted that I would go to the jungle like my grandfather, and I have now met people of these countries.

Sophia: You bring so much gusto to everything, Julio, as if you were totally unafraid, but your art makes me think that you live in a world that vibrates with danger. And to choose to make art, each time, is difficult enough. How do you bring yourself to grab your paintbrush, that snake-birthing snake? Does it scare you?

Julio: Ah! It doesn't scare me, or I think it doesn't scare me, because I am very used to doing it—but there *is* fear there. There is this fear of

seeing what will emerge, what mythical furious demons will appear in my naïve forms of snakes or lions. Because they do emerge, they leak from my unconscious without my noticing. And do sometimes frighten me. But it's a fear I know, an ally. It's what prompts me to keep painting as a way of learning.

Sophia: Years ago you made a portrait of me, and you insisted that I look you in the eyes. Your friend Julia was at your side making a twin portrait, and she also attempted to capture my gaze. The two of you tussled—I loved it—over my gaze. What does the gaze offer you? Is it dangerous like your wildcats? Does it matter when you're not painting a portrait?

Julio: Yes. It all matters. Because a form is a form, after all, a mass of flesh with more or less volume, some shadows, blah blah, but the eyes are infinite wells, doors within, toward the formless within, toward the darkness where everything is held. And to paint the formless is pure alchemy. To head into the mystery of fullness. That's where the venom is. The venom that transforms you and gives you knowledge, a wild knowing that does not pass through the mind. And from that, for me, comes all that art is about. Whether you're painting a portrait by way of some eyes, or the surface of a Chinese vase, if you don't go into the danger and try to translate that unnameable, untouchable thing, the trip's a drag.

Sophia: The gaze is an infinite well and the Chinese vase also has its gaze or equivalent, and I love how you put it. Your vases give me the shivers. You live in Madrid, but you grew up in Toledo, where your parents have an antique shop. Works you've shown over the last few years include golden landscapes, vases, saints, Jesus's face but gold—that is, more than the dream of the forest. Do you, queer and anarchic Julio, hold some passion for the ancient, the royal seal, the Toledan or Castilian? Has your relationship (artistic or in other senses) with Spain changed over the course of your life?

Julio: It has. Patriotism is something I don't understand; I don't have the zeal that many do. Nevertheless, yes, I do feel plenty and, again, in a strange unconscious way, a belonging. A belonging to the Castilian, the Spanish that shapes me. There's this knowledge of the Castilian I've received, I'd say via osmosis, being raised among Castilian antiques, virgins, saints, Jesuses polychromed in gold, urns, objects, objects, objects...When I was younger, I painted in the classical Spanish palette: ochres, reds, earth tones, shadows. After my sojourns to the forest and traveling in chromatically explosive places (like that in which I met you), my colors mutated into neons and I abandoned the classic Spanish tones.

I've disowned much of my antiquarian past—as a child I viscerally rejected it, basically because it was my predetermined fate and not my choice. Now I should make peace with my past, because those colors are coming back, combining harmoniously (or so I intend) with the fluorescents and bling, and all the antique, baroque, Castilian, ancient art of Spain is overpowering me. And I love it!

In your definition as a poet, Sophia, would you include the adjective "American"? Do you feel a sense of belonging to your origins?

Sophia: I do not love my country, and so I do not mean to sound patriotic when I say my poetry is of this country; I do not believe in nations, nor support the policing of borders. However, I grew up reading and listening here, and my poetry is gnarled to that of other U.S. poets at the base, at the most intuitive hypnotized level.

So I do pertain, my poetry pertains to this fucked up imperial death machine of a country. And because of this and the privileges I have been afforded at the expense of others as a "citizen" here, I feel duty-bound to resist capitalism and fascism in the U.S, in a way that I do not feel elsewhere.

Does that resistance inform my poetry? It tries.

I often write dreamily, sleepily, from a sulky trance or luminous confusion or some dark mood leaves me unexpected. I rarely write with intention; nearly never with an idea of what the poem will "say." So my writing is not an efficient form of resistance.

When I write poems that are dreamy, sulky, confused, what I have to do later is distrust them and scrutinize them to make sure they are not dreamily sulkily or confusedly reiterating fascist and capitalist and imperialist logics. Like I had a poem joke that went "where do rainbows go when they've been bad." And the punchline was "prism." And I told it for a while but then stopped because people aren't incarcerated for being "bad."

A friend was like, "Maybe, where do rainbows go when they've been racialized?"

Yes: my poetry belongs to the States, to California, and to Oakland. But it belongs to California dreamily, childishly; to Oakland gratefully, longingly. And to the U.S. grievously, furiously, constantly turning around to see the tyrant.

Julio: You have lived in Spain: have that and other experiences outside the United States changed your way of using words?

Sophia: As I'd never studied ancient languages, learning Spanish (and German, which I don't remember at all anymore) was a linguistic revelation. It allowed me to hear the roots of words. It made me conceive of language as something physical, literal, vegetal. And viral.

And more, I suppose it affected my syntax. It gave me more syntax,

more structures. More commas. I answered your previous question in English; I've responded to this in Spanish. We'll see if it shows in the translation.

Julio: You poets fascinate me, your tools, tools everyone uses daily, and how you use them to extract gold and sustenance from the most insipid: you use your language like a thief breaking into a battleship with a bobby pin, and you manage to bring us to the infinite that seemed dark and bright, to where it's thrilling…why do we create,

Sophia? Is it to combat injustices, each of us feeling that which we have identified? Why do you?

Sophia: Haha. Julioooo. Why do we create, at all? I think my answer is simple, maybe. I like art. I like your paintings. If you didn't make them, I'd miss them. I like poetry. It does help me think, it does give me the chance to name what I love as opposed to that which would devour it, kings, etc. or my own need to be good and pleasing, yes but like I said I don't think it's the only or most efficient way to combat injustice.

I think we like making things, but why poetry, when we could create cake and pie and gardens? Me, maybe I'm not resigned to leaving that dream territory you speak of, that forest of secretive neons. As a kid and tween I believed completely in fairies and other realms: I tried to casually step through mirrors, I stepped in bent grass hoping to be plunged through the earth. As a tween I was more skeptical, but also knew this might be my last chance: while I was in between, while I was not raw dough and not bread. We went camping in the redwoods and I stood in a hollow tree and thought, ok, take me now, if you're ever going to take me. I knew that the other realm was where it was at. This is still art for me, the closest I come. I have a relationship with words. I hear and I see them vividly, they stick in the air, I can circle them. I can pivot them across a page. But they have to come from the danger you speak of, I think, to have that gravity.

When you paint, Julio, when you set out towards the formless, do you go alone? Do you return alone?

Julio: Oh Sophie! I love your questions! Yes, I go alone. And that's a lie: I don't.

I set out alone because I am Julio, a concrete Toledan individual, and I approach it thus. But with this belongingness there are so many, many layers...that is to say, I feel my Castilian belonging very strongly for obvious reasons, but there's also this belonging to humanity. When I see artistic depictions of human history, I feel a thrill that derives from this sense of belonging. I understand things I can't name: when I see Pompeian frescoes, I feel them intimately; when I see cave animals on the walls, they feel familiar to me; the Persian lions speak to me, the Egyptian gods are cousins to me...

I mean, right, the universal is everyone's.

So you make the voyage on your own, but supported and formed by this same universal.

And to return is, I suppose, to rejoin the collective.

Yosefa Raz

Leora Fridman

Yosefa and I spoke while both of us were on "half vacations," as Yosefa termed it, away from our current homes. I was in Berlin and she in Jerusalem, two places moreover that both of us have inhabited but at different times—a category of place that also includes Oakland, California. Never having met in person, we've traced one another's work for a while now, and finally had the opportunity to talk a bit more. —Leora

Leora: Since neither of us is exactly at home, it seems a good way to begin by talking about your relationship to home/land and place.

Yosefa: It's funny, the question of homeland was a burning question—a flaming question in my life for many years. I lived in the States for 15 years, starting in 1999 when I did my MA in Davis, California, then Oakland (where you currently live), and then Toronto, and I was always caught between here and there, and thinking about it a lot, and having two languages (Hebrew and English) and two frames of reference and feeling defensive about both…defensive, ashamed, rich, orphaned, overwhelmed…

But I have to say things have changed since I moved to Tel Aviv, like that whole physical system—like a nervous system, like a certain kind of bone—is gone. The system of longing and nostalgia and home-sickness and yearning, sort of my teenage girl self…telling myself to try and live the questions…

Now I just want to walk down the boulevard and feel the breeze and run into someone I know.

But I also want to say instead of *that* "system" of longing, I have another system in place, which my friend Shaul described as the constant presence/awareness of a sick relative breathing up the air in the room, and that is what it feels like to be Israeli.

Leora: I appreciate that homeland longing can be replaced by other relationships to space, lack thereof or un-wellness.

Yosefa: Yes, apropos sickness, real sickness and metaphorical sickness.

Leora: This makes me think about the move I see often in Oakland by people who are culturally appropriating something. How they say: "I know this is culturally appropriative," nod solemnly, and then they go ahead and do it anyway.

I've been thinking about this in contrast to Israeli-ness, Leftist Israelis I have experienced, and how they hold their politics. The way you described the sick relative, and the lack of air—I think there's a more constant holding of political tension, as opposed to Oakland radicals who too often pick it up and then put it down.

Yosefa: I really like this idea of "holding your politics" like it is a physical ef-fort/practice.

I remember I once went on this week-long peace walk and all these people I knew were there (it was a bit like a dream in that way, because afterwards I also had other important relationships that were only beginning on the peace walk). We went to visit someone's house whose son had died in a terrorist attack and started talking about settlers, and politics. My sister was there (this seems more and more like a dream!) and said something about how our uncle is a settler, but then it was clear that everyone has an uncle who is a settler—all these political questions are tied up in families and intimacy. Maybe it is like that now in the U.S. with Trump, but at the time I thought this was different than how I had experienced things in America.

Leora: Yes, great point! It's so clear in this case that interconnection is an inescapable reality as opposed to a philosophy. And I love hearing about your dream/not dream. A German friend said to me the other day, "I like that you are such a devoted observer." I thought, oh, the romance of observing (and the privilege to observe) and the position of such a thing as devotion, but is that a choice? Whether to be devoted as such? Your story about this peace walk reminds me of this. You do not have a choice there about whether to be devoted.

Yosefa: Yes, the devotion to that "sick relative" too...People here constantly talk about leaving and when to leave, but I am sorry/not sorry to report that I am not leaving.

I was just talking about this at dinner the other night, during what have been endless holiday meals here for the past few weeks, though sometimes good conversations. I was saying that in my twenties these questions about homeland were very big and symbolic. And, of course, all the longing that immigrating brought up for me was in some ways a return to my parents immigration, and their parents' unsettling—like maybe my weird bursts of homesickness in Davis were actually encoded longings for the Poland of my ancestors.

But then in the past few years, the big abstract things got replaced by practical details of partner, job, health...and less the big questions. Also, I really had to just stay somewhere, anywhere, even if it was Kansas or Ottawa. Or Tel Aviv. Just pick a place and not constantly be sad about where I wasn't. And this country was a place I was often summoned to—desired and imposed upon and pulled toward—so I let myself be carried back.

In terms of my work, I do feel a real sense of loss about leaving the Bay Area—it was a moment (in and around Occupy) in which something very intense was happening and I felt the energy of a community of writers around me, and I'm not sure I'll get that again in this life.

And strange that in the past few days I've been dreaming of Canada, of women who I love in Canada bringing me things like poems and tea. In a dream, Helen encouraged me to be a plant, or allowed me to be a plant? I think I learned something there about slow growing,

waiting through different seasons. And Sara and her partner opened up a restaurant in my dream and made me dinner reservations for a celebration. And all the water of Canada, the feeling of non-guilt when flushing the toilet.

Leora: I appreciate, and to some extent long for, the kind of commitment to place you're describing. And politically it makes sense—it is when one stays in the same place for a while that one can actually politically dedicate; though, of course, there can be these intense bursts ("temporary autonomous zones") as you're describing with Occupy.

Going back to the romance and reality of "devotion," I want to ask you about the word specifically. It's a word I think about a lot and have been teaching with, and I remember you used this word in a review of the poet Brandon Brown's work. I'm curious about it relationally, and also in a secular vs religious sense. Is it a word you have a relationship to?

Yosefa: My new-ish life in Israel in some ways feels like it has less room for talk about devotion—because of my relation to religion and politics, as well as my life in the same house with a very secular person. But maybe instead of *talk of devotion,* there are more *acts* of actual devotion. It makes me think of Ruth sticking to Naomi in the Biblical story of two women of different generations and cultures who stick together after death rearranges their lives (maybe that was the context in the BB piece too), she cleaved to her, *davKAH*—from the same root as glue. To make yourself glue on to something, like a country, or a marriage. I guess that is devotion.

Leora: How does this manifest in your work?

Yosefa: For me, these past few years have been years of cleaving to projects—to long unfoldings that are sometimes boring and repetitive, or even painful. I'm doing the opposite of flitting from flower to flower, and I think it shows in my face—a certain kind of tiredness or heaviness maybe.

Maybe I'm trying to do the opposite of immigration, trying to settle in finally, and stand behind my decisions, be firmer even in my flaws and my mistakes. But this all feels unbearably serious, especially for the lightness of a Friday morning in October, first good weather in months, and maybe a movie in the afternoon. Maybe what I'm trying to say is something about the materiality of devotion—you put yourself in a certain place and there you are and it is not another place. I always thought I could somehow transcend place through strong emotion, passion. But I am also working on new metaphors—I have some idea rattling around of crucifixion—dying and being reborn into devotion, dying and being reborn into all my commitments—when all I need is to feel that the earth is holding me back.

Leora: I love this. I turned 33 this year and everyone wanted to call it my "Jesus year. "When I asked my friend Abrah (who identifies as a Hebrew priestess and is very committed to Jewish ancestral work, among other things) what this meant, she said, "It means this year you will be crucified on the altar of something." I did not like this that much, but she went on: "Crucified for a cause—or maybe, for you, for art." Crucifixion as commitment, maybe—noticing at a certain age that I have focused much of my life on a particular thing, and my body has oriented toward, or been laid across and out for, that thing. This "crucifixion," if I have to call it that, is a rare moment for me to have or witness.

Yosefa: Especially re: Bay Area—I often felt there that there wasn't enough glue, people could wander off, you could come if you want but don't come if it doesn't suit you…I wanted people to WANT me to come, to press me to, to be disappointed if I didn't. To be angry at me if I didn't show up.

Leora: Yes! I relate to this very much. I've been teaching this class called "Devotional Writing" and thinking mostly about the act of cleaving. It's surprised me how radical it has felt for me to ask people to cleave to something, and how challenging. Forced cleavage.

Yosefa: Yes, so maybe devotion is very radical in the Bay Area that way, as a mundane kind of practice that has less to do with "spirituality" and more with glue.

Leora: It relates also to this book by the scholar and critic, Jon Nixon, that I'm reading right now, *Hannah Arendt and the Politics of Friendship*. Nixon writes, "Promising, for [Arendt], was not a defensive recoil from the unpredictability of the future—not a way, that is, of transcending, denying or erasing the unpredictable—but an acknowledgement of the fact of that unpredictability: a way of moving forward together into the unbounded uncertainty that constitutes the human condition."

Yosefa: Ah, that's beautiful! I think I'm starting to understand that now that, yes, there is so much unbound uncertainty to contend with, and devotion is not its enemy.

Leora: This kind of commitment through uncertainty came up in your recent interview with David Brazil. You framed the timing of the interview

136

around the Counting of the Omer, the traditional counting of each of the forty-nine days between the Jewish holidays of Passover and Shavuot. Because of this framing in time, the interview had this background of an established, committed practice. I got the impression of you both coming from multiple locations of commitment. To the Omer, to poems, to each other.

Yosefa: I feel like with David, in many ways, we experimented around this idea of devotion, and practice, and *kevah*—things that are constant. David taught me the importance of doing things on a weekly basis, like our weekly *parashah* study (a weekly study of a particular portion of the Bible), which in turn became something to rely on.

Leora: Are there other practices like that in your life these days—in study, in writing or elsewhere that have become similarly devotional?

Yosefa: The nation-state imposes the cycle of the year here—all the holidays—on our lives, and so it is an ongoing practice to try to thrive and find meaning within that cycle. I meditate every morning for a little bit; when I asked a meditation teacher about this little bit, he said if you want to be a little happy meditate a little, if you want to be very happy meditate a lot. So I am practicing being a little happy, a little bit every day. And soon the semester is starting with its schedule of classes—which I am so happy to get to return to year after year. I think this is also a form of love.

Leora: Are you familiar with Laynie Browne's thinking on devotional writing in the magazine *Talisman*? She's one of the few "out" religiously practicing writers I know and have a relationship with. Some time ago she sent me this piece in *Talisman* that she wrote on devotional writing, which largely instructed the Devotional Writing Workshop I've been teaching. It gave me a lot of space in my mind, I think, to be able to consider religious devotion and creative devotion simultaneously.

Yosefa: As a child, my family was religious. I went to Friday night services with my mother every week, and we kept *shabbat* (Sabbath) and separated milk from meat sponges. I'm told I used to keep a bucket under my bed so I could do ritual hand washing the moment I woke up, and I was always drawn to religious figures, like my first grade teacher who wore a wig and taught us to pray with devotion. I was Mother Rachel in a school play, and there were special lights that made the white of my robes glint and shimmer.

Yosefa: Many of the writers I study and talk with are religious, even if it is in some complicated insider-outsider, love-hate way. I'm thinking of Maria Melendez Kelson, who I met in my first years in America, and now my friendship with Amital Stern, a writer who is deeply immersed in the abjection and monstrosity of religious Jerusalem, Jerusalem as monster and Goddess. And in my scholarship, I write about the prophetic voice—writers like Abiezer Coppe, William Blake, Walt Whitman, Haim Nachman Bialik…though secretly I am quite resistant to prophecy.

I can't talk about Hebrew thought and Jewish meditation the way that Laynie Browne does. It's too immersed and tainted in the drama of Zionism for me to come at it from a peaceful place. And kabbalistic practices are also entangled with modern day messianism; I guess that is the luxury of coming to kabbalah and Jewish meditation in America: you don't have to listen to all these messianic strains, you can just turn off that channel.

My parents left (and recently came back) to religion, so I was left a bit in the cold with it—more insider/outsider, more, as we say in Hebrew, *at the threshold of the lock* (which is a quote from Song of Songs and the modern Hebrew writer Shmuel Yosef Agnon). That said, I do feel that through my biblical scholarship I have made some sort of deal with this longing. I have made myself a little space of knowledge and authority I am comfortable with.

Leora: After reading your interview with David, I was left considering how spirituality does or doesn't interact with contemporary American poetics. How so few people claim actual public identities involving religion, but then many poets and readers are obsessed with tarot, CA Conrad's rituals, and the like.

Yosefa: Right, the difference between religion and spirituality. There's something embarrassing about religion, about its specificity—the matriarchs and the patriarchs—not to mention, the whole God thing. And then you have to donate money, "tithe," or pay for your seat in the Yom Kippur services. And you have to reckon with all the crazies…

I think "spirituality" is a more elegant way of managing those feelings and affects without as much commitment. And less scars. But this goes back to the question of devotion and heaviness—I'm still trying to figure this one out. The balance of lightness and heaviness. What you can show on your skin.

Leora: Yes, beautiful. I have to some extent come (back) to practicing spiritual forms within Judaism in recent years because I want to be somehow authentically devoted, responsibly devoted. I think also as a white person in and around Black-led movements in the Bay Area, I've had a number of POC remind me how crucial it is to look to my own lineage as opposed to that of others.

Yosefa: I have to remember all these questions of cultural appropriation and the language around them, that doesn't come up as often here, or in different ways (maybe because there is actually a lot more appropriation, of land, of water, etc).

Leora: Yes, definitely. Going back to poetics, I'd love to hear more about your thinking on prophets and poets—which I know you think about mostly because I've really appreciated that you publicly share your teaching syllabi on these topics online!

Yosefa: I'm really struck by the connection between prophetic sign acts and Conrad's somatic rituals—the way a body can put itself in the path of Empire, even when the proportions between Empire and one body are of such different proportions that it is ridiculous. The way prophets did crazy things like walk naked, lie on their side, cut off their beard and divide it into three parts, bury a loincloth, break a pot.

Scholars usually classify these "sign acts" as didactic or pedagogical—Jeremiah breaks a pot to make a greater impression on his audience. But many of them have no audience, take a long time to perform, don't really have a clear message.

I'm thinking of Conrad's ritual around the Iraq War and wearing a catheter, or putting broken glass in their shoe. Nobody sees that; it's not educational. I love teaching the rituals/poems/exercises to students because they unravel that educational momentum, or the directionality of the mimetic/symbolic and invite you into another way of making meaning. The Biblical prophet Hosea has to marry a prostitute. You give up or transform your whole life in service of a message or idea, but when you come close to it that idea breaks down into something incomprehensible. Which is what happens in war, or crisis, or what we are living through now. Great incomprehensible changes, and we can respond with our bodies.

And yes, sharing the syllabi. That feels like my move against the "capitalism of knowledge" to quote my teacher Chana Kronfeld. I often get help with syllabi, it's my favorite kind of Facebook, so it seems only right that I put it back into the common space. Sometimes I feel syllabi are my favorite genre of writing. They are all potential, all connections waiting to happen, and these connections that happen in class discussion are sometimes so ephemeral, something magical happening in class that it is really hard to go back and

140

	explain later, that feeling of thinking together, and having emotions together.
Leora:	As a reader of syllabi, I often feel I am a voyeur on that feeling of thinking together. I can't quite see behind the curtain, but I know what might be happening somewhere due to the text I'm reading at the moment.
Yosefa:	Also, the main literary device of the syllabus is juxtaposition. Like CA Conrad and Jeremiah. Maybe because of being from two countries and also always replicating that—two languages, two academic disciplines, two cities I move between—the classroom (and the syllabus) seem like the utopian place where you put those things together and they make sense in some ecstatic intellectual moment that can't be replicated. (Not that teaching is always like that!)
Leora:	Definitely not! But the everlasting search for it is real. The ecstatic is another theme I see consistently in your work, along with the disappointment involved in existing alongside the search for the ecstatic. I see in your work something I connect to other poets of Occupy Oakland: a piling-on, a constant over-fullness, a desire for complete inclusion of experience, specifically including mess. Does this feel like an accurate association? And was it something happening in your work prior to your time in Oakland?
Yosefa:	The ecstatic is from before Occupy Oakland, from growing up in/ alongside the majesty and abjection of Jerusalem and its constant stream of excessive mystics. Various members of my family who crossed continents and lost their homes and languages in order to be part of something bigger. My father told me that I wanted to be part of Jewish history. But when you go to Jerusalem it's so disappointing always—the garbage and the petty politics (the smallness of the Jordan river as metonymic of this) and the racism and homophobia of the people you want to admire. And the army behind it all, clearing a space for the mystics to pray.
	This is something from a piece I'm working on about a documentary by Moran Ifergan about the Western Wall: "The women on screen pray and cry instead of me. I turn to you, in the cold movie theatre, my arm on your bare leg. I didn't plan this, I whisper, but it's as if

141

the movie is speaking to us, about the terrible failures of faith inside a marriage, the ways your heart can't bear to love. And this is the secret root of everything, the women crying, alone, the soldiers with their stupid rallies and all the dirt and fear of Jerusalem. This is the heart of the matter."

Well, that's just more mess—marriages and weeping—but maybe they belong with the mystics. I feel like my mother told me, *don't be too much, too loud, too fat, too weepy.* Or maybe, more accurately, she feared that *she* was too much. And my first poetry teacher in a very different way had an aesthetics of restraint, of minimalism. Maybe also a way for her to survive in the too-much of Jerusalem. A lot of subtlety, secrets on the page. A lot of cutting words out—this was her devotion. And lots of Hebrew poetry, especially by women, has an aesthetics of minimalism, of impoverishment, of simplicity.

But I'm not like that at all, and I can't help the way my memories of the army, for instance, came to me like some kind of colorful, baroque, grotesque animation. Over-saturated. Which is why I filtered my life in the army through Henry Darger scenes. But yes, overdoing it, like Dodie Bellamy, Stephanie Young, and Sheila Heiti (who I know you've written about), as well as writers here like Tahel Frosh and Sheikha Helawy (I've translated a bit of both). Writers who have given themselves over to the over-doing, to maximalism, to taking up space on the page and in life.

Sheila Heti has a passage about female genius in *How Should a Person Be* about how no one knows what that might look like. Yet, to me, there seems to be female genius in these commitments—maybe we could call it devotions—to excess, to mess, to truth-telling. But you still have to be clever about it. It is a performance.

Leora: I've been reading Susan Best on affect in feminist contemporary art, and she writes about performance that lets the reader be alongside of the work, instead of overwhelmed by it: "The sense of restraint or the introverted emotional tone of the works means that the beholder is drawn alongside the work rather than being drawn into it...a respectful non-intrusive being with." I like this *alongside.* Of course, I relate to what you're saying around the socialized aversion to too-muchness—and I think Best is pointing to a muchness that still allows for the muchness of others to still exist. A relational muchness. This reminds me of how I am often asking someone *how are you doing* at an art opening or poetry reading, and really wanting to know. But it's usually uncomfortably received. Perhaps it's a sense that any affect we experience should stay contained in the work we are making. And it's also gendered, asking about FEELINGS. I've wondered this here in this conversation: We don't know each other all that well, and amongst all these questions part of me just wants to ask: *How is your body? How are you feeling?*

Yosefa: I know, this is a funny conversation to be having so dis-embodied, and I find myself longing to be at that art opening or poetry reading and have that kind of conversation with you! This is a first for me— being interviewed. But it seems an extension of how I write too—my fantasy of being interviewed, or questioned, by curious people who wish me well! Though that fantasy, of being asked by my "American friends" or "American lovers" about Israel or Israel/Palestine ended up going in some perverse directions in the poetry I wrote in America.

Leora: Perverse directions! Yes please! I'm thinking of your recent work in *Elderly*. These lines stick with me: "mannequins without heads are singing this call to arms / call these legs and tell them you're running late." I feel I'm calling those legs in our dis-embodied state. But we're getting long here, and running late, so we'll stop for now. Thank you!

Ana Karen G. Barajas

+

Vreni Michelini Castillo

Ana Karen and I are both from the state of Guanajuato, a conservative leaning state located in the central part of Mexico. Currently, Guanajuato has one of the highest homicide rates, with femicides being a large portion of those deaths. For this reason and a multitude of other pressures, Guanajuato has a large migrant population. Ana Karen and I crossed paths more than 10 years ago through our past loves (who are brothers). Throughout the last decade, we have continued connecting through our love for music, art, and our embodiment of a new type of womynhood that defies the norms of our state.

For this project, we talked through videos and texts on Instagram chat. We decided to share our conversation through photography and poetry, reflecting our art practice and recent migrations. Ana Karen sent her pieces first and I replied. —Vreni

<u>Sonaba con "la."</u>

Lo sombrío pasa
mientras recuerdo lo nuevo.
Lo que se siente,
los pasatiempos, las palabras.
Lo que parece estar firme
se vuelve volátil
la duda, la lejanía
me impide recordar
como era el ahora
y lo que algún día
parecía ser importante
para mi,
de mi,
de los que observan.
Ahora creo
que me fui tal vez huyendo
pero le agradezco
a la huida
ya no sueno con la misma nota
y no se si pueda regresar a ello.

Fantasma soy

Desde que estoy aquí
siento que soy fantasma.
He cambiado de cuerpo
también lo he dejado
no me ven.

Hay algunos otros
que me pueden ver
por que ven otras dimensiones
y otros que,
aun que no me vean
me pueden sentir,
los puedo tocar,
susurrarles en sueños
y jalarles los pies.

A veces estar invisible
se vuelve como estar
en una tina llena de agua,
no me quiero salir.

—Ana Karen

Semiamarga

El ir y venir
es un privilegio
un camino abierto
que pocos gozan

saboreo esa libertad

el aroma tan único de la cocina de
mi abuelita
arte que surge de las sobras
creatividad de nuestro pueblo

entre sorbitos, palabras semiamar-
gas

cuchillito

muestran tanto nuestra herida
gente bonita, gente torturada por la
negación

…intento trazar,
continuar esas conversaciones que
duran años

amamanto esas amistades que me
han visto desgarrarme
solo pa' allarme después,
mas perra, mas ligera

me apoyo en nuestros apapachos
nuestra confianza
esa complicidad
momentos tenues que se evaporan

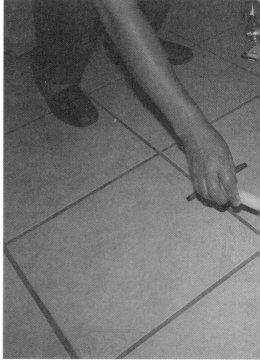

al cruzar migración

mis manos escurriendo de ansiedad
que más me pueden quitar?

siempre he sido muy sensible
de niña vomitaba bilis al sentirme tra-
icionada,
desilusionada…
algo que me pasa hasta la fecha
pa' quitarme los empachos emocionales
me enfoco mas y mas en el pasado,
aunque duela saber como mis abuelas
fueron violentadas

tierra escurriendo sangre

necesito enfrentar esos murmullos
escuchar mis tormentas
imaginarme
esos mil caminos que cruzaron

trato de rascar la memoria de mis may-
ores
de quien me escuche

se que soy lo que no quieren ver

la mezcla violenta

trato de buscarles en mis sueños
ahí es donde encuentro respuestas

duermo poco
sueño mucho

viajo en el ciclo del tiempo
sacudiendo el polvo
en el que nos enterraron

veo mis muertes

siento el porvenir

—V. Michelini Castillo

Photographs taken by Ana Karen: 1. Shiijiazhuang desde las alturas (image with buildings) 2. Buitrago (image with trees) 3. Gris. (above)

Photographs taken by V. Michelini Castillo during Aguas Migrantes 2nd Artist Residency: 1. Guanajuato 2. Michoacan, Mexico, 2017. Aguas Migrantes is a migrant artist collective co-founded by V. and Susa Cortez in 2015. www.aguasmigrantes.org Instagram. @aguasmigrantes

Claire Buss

+

Hannah Kingsley-Ma

I met Claire my sophomore year of college. She lived in the same ramshackle farmhouse on a haunted prairie at the edge of campus the year before I did, and as a result the two of us became friends. She was always starting stuff—joining bands, running the college radio station, creating a zine that involved most of our friends. The zine was called "The Miracle Suit," and it was so much fun to make. Late at night we would take over two basement printers in the library and print a tower of copies that we would pass out the next day in the cafeteria. She had this way of getting everyone involved that seemed effortless. It was a collaborative effort but it also carried her clear sense of ambition and taste—her droll sense of humor, her emotional precision, her keen appetite for straight-faced absurdity.

Long after we graduated the two of us continued to write emails to one another. Claire writes great emails. They are shapely, and funny, and I like that we are both performing a little for one another—writing in a way that we know the other will like. Since graduating college, Claire's been working as a filmmaker in Seattle. She's also the creator and host of a participatory, live game show called The Future is Zero. *It started as a project Claire and her best friend Kat hatched in their living room. Since then it has expanded to the Northwest Film Forum, and is wholly elaborate. I had the chance to see it a couple of months back and was blown away by it. It was so joyful and deranged and assuredly made. When Claire's on stage she's not Claire Buss. She's CLAY BUFF. Clay Buff wears the same gold sequined minidress and shouts things like JUICE HER UP. Contestants have to do things like guess YouTube trends to draw "teen blood" from an idling teenager, hooked up to a fake IV (whoever gets the most blood wins), or search through a pile of Amazon boxes to search for the elusive "golden employer paid health insurance card." I struck up our email correspondence again to ask her about how she makes the show. —Hannah*

Claire: This is a great excuse to get back into our email habit. I was curious and looked through some old correspondences with you and saw an email exchange between us from 2011 and I start the email with "dear kingslut." 2011 was a...different time.

The Future is Zero is a surreal, satirical game show in Seattle that features artists from different disciplines competing against each other in a series of challenges in front of a live studio audience. It's been called "Double Dare for depressed people." It's a mix of physical games and bizarre trivia about feeling like the world is ending, set in a kind of PeeWee's Playhouse dreamworld. We built a 10 foot tall, 170 pound television for our most recent show and it played animations over the contestants' heads. We were all really worried that it would accidentally fall and crush someone and damn, what a crazy way that would be to die.

I started the project four years ago in my living room here in Seattle as a kind of DIY art experiment, and we'd invite local bands to come on, and we lined the halls of the house with this red felt to make it feel like a set. It was a serious fire hazard and the most fun. I made the show after watching a ton of old game shows during a really wet winter. I love the retro-futuristic set design on some of those older shows and some of the game formats and ideas are so bonkers and feel really innovative to me.

Hannah: My experience of going to your show was that I felt really taken care
of. That's kind of my favorite experience of art, where you are im-
mersed in something weird and dynamic but also are quickly assured
that this thing is going to be really good, and well-made, and meant
to be experienced by people. There seems to be a really masterful
combination of breathless ambition and thoughtfulness in the work
that you make—thoughtfulness in terms of taste, and humor, and
how the whole thing is going to function as a whole. And it's kind of
crazy because there are all these moving parts in the game show! Do
you have a set of aesthetic principles you try and follow when dream-
ing this crazy thing up? What are the instincts you've developed that
help guide you, in terms of making things that you know are good but
also are reasonable for the for the kind of production work you do?

Claire: I'm glad you felt taken care of at the show you attended. Making sure
the audience is having a good time is the most important thing to me.
Like, a stranger decided to leave their house and buy a ticket to see
your thing, when they could have been at home watching television,
or eating yogurt, or whatever it is people with free time do. You can't
take it for granted that people want to see your art, so you owe it
to them to be ambitious and put your whole self into it and make it
good.

Kat and I have gradually built the sensibility of the show and refined
it over the past several years, so at this point I feel like we know what
we like and what we think is funny. An important thing to me is inten-
tion even when we're doing a bit that is aggressively stupid. I don't
like things that are weird just for weird sake, or like some Burning
Man shit. I want everything we do to have a reason for being there.
Some of the more outlandish things we've done include: trapping our
contestants in a micro-studio built live on stage, an elaborate flash-
back narrative that involved a 1950s set sitting on top of our regular
set, a high school drumline surprising the audience with a very long
digression, a too-long ode to Las Vegas, and unleashing a wet dog
to run through the audience.

Hannah: I feel like the definitive quality of a gameshow is audience participation. How did you know you wanted to make participatory art? And is there something you get from involving the audience that you think is lost on the rest of us, who present whatever we are making to a faceless crowd and then walk away from it?

Claire: I feel like I came to the audience participation element because I was playing in a bunch of bands at the time and my life kind of revolved around going to and playing shows. I was dating the lead singer in my band and he used to kind of lose his shit on stage in this really electric, unhinged way, and I always envied that. Women aren't encouraged to do that! Hosting the show was my way of being able to lose my shit on stage in a really cathartic way, but also in a way that invites people in and allows them to empathize with these feelings of despair that we focus on in the show. You don't have to be some genius artist to feel like you're going insane. Being alive right now is the act of feeling fucking insane everyday.

Hannah: It's really interesting to me that you talk about the show as a way of mirroring a kind of collective insanity, because the show itself is so produced—like wonderfully, and expertly so, which is to say it feels really in control. I wonder if this balance is the sweet spot, it's the role of silliness. You're twisting the edges of reality but winking and saying: We know what we're doing! We're doing it on purpose! Because I am not sure I would like it if I was watching something and someone just went totally unhinged without that wink. I think that would make me uncomfortable. But also I am not that fun, have no interest in traveling to outer space, and today while getting my flu shot asked the nurse practitioner to look at my ear because it "felt red" so maybe that's just a ME thing.

Claire: That production value is all Kat, to be honest. I feel like I bring a lot of the ideas and energy to this thing, but Kat and the rest of the production team actually bring it to life and make it look good and professional. After working with teams of people in general while making films, you learn to keep each other accountable for high production value and really going for it. It's hard for me to imagine making something totally by myself anymore. When you're alone, you have no one to tell you when a joke is stale, or that you can try harder at something, or to give you the encouragement to keep going. I've written scripts about things that are very personal to me, but by abstracting it and involving a team, it allows some necessary distance and morphs into this collective work.

Do you feel like the performative aspect of the literary world gives you a similar sense of catharsis? That to me is what makes me feel sane these days. An expression of what's going on inside seeping to the outside.

Hannah: I feel like recently with my writing, the kind of performance I'm trying

to enact is a plain vulnerability. I love autofiction, whatever that word means. And I love funny writing that intertwines humor with sadness and where all the lines have the resonance of a joke. And so I've just been trying to write these embarrassing stories that pull from some kind of observed incidence in my life and leave in the bits that make me cringe. And maybe that's the other side of the coin to getting on stage and saying FUCK IT!! and losing your shit. I feel like there is this gendered aspect to it. Like I should be convincing the men I want to impress that I exclusively think about Knausgaard. But I don't feel like I should be out here proving it to you that I'm smart for you to assume that I'm not vapid. I used to worry that writing about certain things would undermine my authority, do nothing to Advance the Cause of Women in the Eyes of Literary Men. But the thing I'm really interested in writing about is the differing textures of intimacy, between sisters and romantic partners and close friends. And I don't really care if it alienates male readers who find it trivial. I'm getting my MFA right now and I feel like all the men are like: I gotta right something that feels HONEST and aims to capture the TRUTH and I'm just not about that. My sense of scale is different, and I'm pushing up against that right now in school.

It's still a persona I enact though. It's not really me, it's a version of me. And you have a version of you in this show, this crazy alter-ego CLAY BUFF.

Claire: I guess the Clay Buff version of me is a little more showy and ego-maniacal. The alter ego thing just started a way for me to distance myself from the reality of actually being on stage doing these ridiculous things. Now that I'm less embarrassed by it all, the persona is a useful way to think about performance of identity. We're all doing it all the time anyway, so an alter ego doesn't seem that outlandish anymore.

Magic Jewelry aura photos, NYC, fall 2016
The interpreter said the white spots on the bottom right side of Amanda's photo (left) were our pure relationship.

From **Institutional Language**: *If it's easier to do this through email that's fine, too, but perhaps a quick discussion would be best? Please let me know what you'd prefer.*

Amanda Davis

+

Kate Robinson Beckwith

Culled from emails, texts, video transcriptions, and personal files, the hybrid text here is an accretion of nearly 15 years of friendship. A marker in time to elucidate how our correspondence has shaped us. Creating is in so many ways a supremely personal experience, but for each of us the dialogue with each other and others that comes out of the creative act and supports it is what keeps us engaged.—Kate

Nov 27, 2007, 2:14 PM

Amanda Davis <luckynbr9@yahoo.com>
To: kate robinson <raisetheshade@gmail.com>

Hey dude,

I totally rambled on these questions but didn't care to edit. (sorry)...

1) What does the word identity mean to you as an artist?

Identity to me as an artist has two almost contradicting roles that go hand in hand. One role is its ability to set one apart from the world, to create a "screen" or "wall" for the artist so they can uniquely process the world around them. It's in that observer-like position that I find an artist creates the need for art, as a means to cross that wall or screen. To set up a dialog with the outside world either physically or unconsciously. And in that behavior sets up a subjective personality of an artist as an individual (see answer to question #3.) The other role that identity has is its ability to create inclusiveness for the artist to their sought out community. Which leads directly to the next question you asked.

Thinking now more than ever this is inherent in how some-
one "becomes" an "artist." Simply put...
They consciously and/or unconsciously can't process the
world without creating.

2) What role has community played in shaping your identity as an artist?

The role that community has made in shaping my identity as an artist is infinite. You said it best when you described art as an onion. Layers build on layers, etc. (I hope you remember what I'm talking about. We were both high on coke...) Basically I have created my own style from adopting other artists' styles. A (healthy) community creates the ability to build layers. Which in turn can create a distinctive style in art where artists share specific common philosophies, styles or goals. Warhol's factory created Warhol just as much as Warhol created his factory. However, we both know what a double-edged sword "community" can be. It can both nurture and destroy creativity. Community has to have boundaries, competition, sharing, growth etc. and has to have the capacity to understand each other in order to be a nurturing community.

I'm glad I'm not in my 20's.

I don't agree with this example any longer.
I don't particularly care about Warhol either.

I wonder how this really takes foot in large-
scale capacities? I.e the "institution."

3) What (if any) identity would you give yourself as an artist?

Who knows. Who cares. No offense to your question. I find the more I put my art out there that more I get feedback of what my "identity" is. I do the same to other artists. At Otto's right now there's all this crazy psychedelic art up and I assume this person who painted it is a dude who's really into drugs, wears tie-dye and is a trippy sort of person. I don't know him/her/it. But I've already given them an identity. Most of the time the viewer misses the point or comes up with one that the artist didn't even think of. Maybe Thomas Kinkade is painting the downfall of American civilization, and is really cool?

Aww. Remember Otto's?
They're re-opening!

I believe now, looking back...
that he was.

Sorry I wrote way too much but Jesse was sleeping and I didn't have anything to do. And you know how much I like projects.

I love you, come home soon,
Amanda

Oct 15, 2010, 6:20 PM
Amanda Davis <luckynbr9@yahoo.com>
To: kate robinson <raisetheshade@gmail.com>

This feels like too much and not enough at the same time.

Oh well, here you go:

Nostalgia	Dank	Ridiculous	Cultivate
Formation	Porous	Mighty	Constant
Poignancy	Sound	Solitude	Bond
Empathy	Chilling	Over-thinking	Pouring
Amazement	Awkward	Haggard	Green
Absorption	Attachment	Complicated	Grey
Waterlogged	Voyeurism	Heart	Hairy
Radicalism	Overwhelming	Blood	Complex
Mold	Naivete	Tears	Change
Transient	Glare	Bare	Knowledge
Humor	Tethered	Noise	Stupidity
Immense	Forging	Patience	Small
Limitless	Weirdo	Limited	Drunk
Frustration	Easy	Worth	
Passion	Sexy	Janky	

10/15/18
Kate:

I remember feeling so enamored with an idea
I had of community that never fully cohered,
except for in my head.

It's interesting to have left that place, the physical
place, Olympia, but also the emotional place
where I was so certain my little community of
misfits was what would save me.

I have been thinking about this a lot since my
dad passed in February. Part of this is realizing he
taught me this community building compulsion.

To clarify, I don't mean that I was wrong about my community being the thing that saves me, just that I had no idea, at the time, what "saving" really meant, or what exactly we were being saved from, aside from a diffuse feeling of the fuckedness of the world.

10/15/18
Kate: Since then I've gone to graduate school, become enmeshed with "real" poets, been pepper sprayed by the police at Occupy, shut down the port, watched home-lessness rise sharply, endured severe work trauma, had my friends die in a national tragedy, gotten married, and had my father drop dead for no apparent reason other than what I'd call a "failure to thrive"

I didn't even mention Trump. Well, now I have.

12/6/11
Amanda:

Today I walked from lower Manhattan to Midtown with the sole purpose of buying a good fork, knife and spoon. I've actually been living in the city now for 5 months and have yet to buy any eating utensils.

Walking around the city, I'm reminded of the frenzied, romantic feeling I started here with. Admittedly though, the feeling has lessened to become a more reasonable under-standing that this place is now part of my new real life.

I sometimes mouth the words "how am I here?"

To understand direction truly, is to know that movement is so much more jagged and complicated than the "linear" transition of one thing to the next thing.
I had you all along. I have you all along.

"How am I not here?" I live with all my great loves.

I guess I don't feel solidly like I'm living here because I've forgotten how to attach myself to that idea of a solid place. There's so much more that lives with me in this place than what exists on this coast.

I can't remove any of it. The direction I'm moving is moving with all those other direc-tions. The further I go to point A, the further I go from Point B, simultaneously though, they edge in closer

I am here. I am there.

I take you everywhere I go.

10/15/18
Kate:

Accumulation is the most enduring. I've taken you so many places at this point, but

Remember when your parents' moving van got scammed and it sat in some unknow
ment to things, now I'm obsessed with letting go.

You've always been a better minimalist than me

Jul 29, 2012, 10:12 AM
Amanda Davis <luckynbr9@yahoo.com>
To: kate robinson <raisetheshade@gmail.com>

I'm sending this to you before I forget.

Enjoy Olympia.
I'll see you in New York

Written on 4/15/12
She is a thing of beauty. No eye could ever understand. Since in those details, those marks, subtle in their form, furnish a spectacle that tackles the purest
fragrance of all the worthiest of human endeavors. She is fervor within fever

Infallible

She is human experience

Because she knows better and resolves to knowing no worse.

The most romantic notion is not to create her above all else but to sense the half-a-second which within a second she contemplates her being and let her be.

Since even in the times which are least likely to be holding a thoughtful reverence, she moves with it in steadiness.

to imagine myself not having the full kitchen I've amassed here in Oakland after 8 years.

ge space in Olympia until it inevitably was auctioned off? Of course you do. At the time I had such an attach-

9/18/12
Amanda:

The thing that couldn't hold, resolved to find the kindest structure for us all.
I know you'll be fine
since I've known you better than anyone

It is this thing above all else that had its name before us

In question we asked to see something different and within that there was no sight worthwhile.

We had to close our eyes and know we wouldn't see again

It is that thing that had a name
lovers
friends
family

It is the thing that had a substance
place
and
time

there is no guessing anymore what this would be like
there is no other lifetime that had a chance

Mar 3, 2013, 10:11 PM
Amanda Davis <amabdavis@gmail.com>
To: kate robinson <raisetheshade@gmail.com>

This is our collaboration, maybe a book. The idea of alone,
separation, union, bi-coastal. In form of a conversation.
I see it as something printed like a diptych. Like two tin cans
on the end of a very long string.

Yes?

Sometimes this city is loud and hard and quiet and soft and sometimes it has you and sometimes it doesn't.

4/29/15   6/2/09
Amanda: Kate:

I have nothing to say. I am adult. I commute. I get up early.

All for the other well, there are always so many things to cry about.

Forge the ending or beginning

I want to move in this thing with intelligence i say too much, usually, to people that i care about. or people i think

With grace i care about. people i want to care about. people i think i want to care

I'm learning to be forceful about. sometimes i say to much. in the desire to be honest, sometimes

High demands i say too much.

And to breathe

What that sounds like

And to sleep enough it's ok. it's a consistent characteristic that i am learning how to deal with.

but sometimes it results in tears.

i do too much, usually, activities i care about getting done. people
i want to do them with.

everyone is working. or living, trying to live, trying to float. and shining,
despite clouds. so many clouds. appearing from nowhere sometimes.

and succeeding. magically! as the sun has set and still darkness hasn't
captured.

again, sometimes resulting in tears.

Mar 1, 2018, 11:10 AM
Amanda Davis <amabdavis@gmail.com>
To: Kate Robinson <raisetheshade@gmail.com>

I was just looking up something unrelated in my Gmail account and came across this—with slight chills for how awesome our lives have been and are.

One more for the archive!

---------- *Forwarded message* ----------
From: soul lives <soullives@hotmail.com>
Date: **Mon, Feb 21, 2005 at 11:11 PM**
Subject: Ladyfest Band Committee Minutes for 2/20/5

In Attendance:
Lily, Kate, Shannon, Amanda, Beth, Jenny, Shizuno, Domenica, Erika

Beth takes minutes at next meeting on 6th March at 1pm at Amanda & Kate's (303 Division St)

Went over our lists of Bands we'd like to see come to Ladyfest. The following lists are of bands mentioned only once. Sorry if I spell any wrong or goof?

[INTERMINABLE LIST OF BANDS TO SOLICIT FOR LADYFEST OLYMPIA]

Between now and the next meeting, we are expected to begin contacting bands and find out who might be interested. Kate and Amanda will start work on a packet and letterhead to send to interested bands. It may include the Time magazine article about last Ladyfest.

Fundraising for the mailing may begin soon, including a night at the Brotherhood in March.

Tabled submissions subcommittee discussion, but talked about an open mic talent show occurring a few weeks before the festival.

Agenda for next meeting:
Review letter and packet.
Check-in on contacts made.

9/12/18
Kate:
The only thing we've done that comes close to Ladyfest and dancing to Barbara Lynn is banging rocks and vocalizing for Pauline Oliveros by the East River, delirious from lack of sleep cause of NYABF '14

09/17/18
Kate:

Some days I get paralyzed by how many different things I want to do. More days than not these days, if I'm being honest.

I keep thinking about the word "correspondence" and its duality. Corresponding, we are, sending transmissions across a country, but also twinned, in relation to one another, bound. What's a dictionary definition of this particular meaning?

I was searching through my emails to find the furthest back point of our email correspondence and got sidetracked by the email containing Caleb's and my combined astrological chart I spent my last dollars on on a bus from Philadelphia to NYC two days after we met. Do you know the exact time of your birth? Why have I never looked into our combined chart?

I know yr terribly busy this month with work. I wonder if you ever have working moments that don't feel totally like work, that somehow transcend it; I hope so. I imagine so? If even just moments, ultimately what you're doing is connecting people, which I think is at the root of why you'd ever wreck yourself for it. Why we do or why one of our tribe ever would. That and the spectre of achievement. Also financial ruin.

My mom said the other day "it's just money" and I almost wept with appreciation.

I hope I'm making sense, but I know I am. To you.

Your birthday present is burning a hole in my pocket.

As I've had a harder and harder time responding to her last email my mom and I have been texting more. Almost as if the fact of the higher level (deeper self) correspondence being undertaken on one plane has opened the flow of traffic on a separate register. One could call it more superficial, small talk, and I guess, though it can be quite intimate, rather, this is where intimacy is built sometimes now that we're tethered to our phones. I'm writing this to you on my phone. For better or worse my phone has shaped most of my closest relationships these days, including that of my neck-to-shoulder-to-elbow

Hellooooo

Iiiiiiii

Miss you

I'm in rehearsals

All this week

So

Been just

Kind of

Slowly losing my mind

In a good way

I like it when I actually work on shows rather than pre-plan for things that will ultimately, uh,
not
be worth planning. Um. It's always really funny cause it's like, y'know, if you are a good
producer that means that no one notices the work that you do, right? So, like, if you're a bad
producer, yes, it's very noticeable,
but if you actually do a good job none of it can be seen. So.

Uh

Anyways

I

It is noon

and I have not

gotten dressed yet

ummmm

and my phone is at 22% battery

aaaand

I finally stopped crying

but

that's how I feel today

I have to re- *sniffs*

write my Mother Jones fellowship cover letter

because

need to

um

maybe not re-write

I need to, like

tinker with it

to

include some

something about this

Am very excited

To

Um

Hear

About

All these th

Er

I am

I am h

Am excited to have heard about all these

I am losing

I can't do this

I cannot actually record this

I wonder

I'm gonna delete this b'cause I cannot speak

I've been working

I just worked 12 hours

I just can't

I'm so tired

Kavanaugh

thing

I dunno

what

yet

I have to write it first

um

I hope yr doing ok

voice cracks

They just hate us so much

sniffs

It's like so fucked

and I just like

knew

I knew

we know

have always known

sniffs

10/10/18
Kate:

Yesterday when I discovered my old Livejournals it was truly horrifying, but, as I said over text, also magnificent, compelling. Especially considering I've been thinking a lot lately about the early days of the internet, and their impact on me, these journals span such a long period (2001-2009), the tipping point for the internet, I think. I'm also so mortified by the spiral of my existence, how despite how much I've changed since 2001 (the journal starts in the spring semester of my senior year of high school) in so many ways my concerns are still the same. Or my emotional struggles are, my existential struggles, it's the repetition with difference pattern. The journal shows my most abject self, too, and I marvel at how willingly I showed myself to my readership, ie. "the public," even if it was just a list of friends.

Fran misses you.

Philip Koščak

+

Chelsea A. Flowers

Correspondence is a powerful force. It's the reaching out to acknowledge someone. Even with the slightest form of communication, that action matters. You can be right next door, or thousands of miles away it makes a difference. It's an act of acknowledging one's humanity. In a series of conversations in the present, and revisiting old texts from the past, I present the work of Philip Koščak.—Chelsea

Chelsea: Long time no speak. In preparation for this conversation I looked back to the earliest text that I have from you in my phone. It's from March 17th, 2017. I know I have earlier texts but my phone is dumb, and that is as far back as it goes. The text you sent is of a funny/stupid image. Looking back at this peculiar early text, I'm realizing that it really encapsulates you as a person and your art practice. Let's get a working definition: How would you describe your work?

Philip: It doesn't have to make sense. If it looks good, eat it. Please don't leave me. Byeeeeeeeeee.

Chelsea: That's a funny description, it's like a Tweet. I think that's super interesting because you're conveying these themes in such delicate actions. And I feel like your use of materiality is super interesting. This is no shade, or criticism, it's just an observation but, it feels like the use of fabric to create weird shit is the current trend in the Midwest. I've seen so many Midwestern, specifically fem-identifying artists, working within fabric and ideas of Camp, Kitsch, and Trumploy, which is a whole 'nother conversation in and of itself. But when I think about your work I don't relate it to my opinion of the "current Midwestern aesthetic" And so I am curious about your choice of materials?

Philip: That is interesting to hear about this from a Midwesterner's perspective because I always thought of the quick campy kitschy materials as a very LA thing but hearing that, maybe it's more universal than I thought. In general, most of the materials I choose are readily available and can be manipulated fairly easy without shop tools. I'm domestic. It's important for me to be able to edit and alter as I go. The recreation and labor involved with many of the installations and sculptures is a large part of the process too. I hope that my labor put into manipulating the familiar/readily available/cheap materials transforms into wonder when someone views the final work.

And yeah the fem and queer artists working in fibers is a whole other convo, but like many of those artists, I gravitate towards the soft material because they are bodily.

Chelsea: So speaking of the "A word" aesthetics, do you feel like there is an LA aesthetic?

Philip: Yes and no. I disagree when people assume LA is solely "Pop." It's usually hard to convince them since my work has a lot of pop culture references but there's so much more. There's a lot of experimental stuff going on right now especially in the digital, new media, and social practice realms so it'd be hard for me to describe an aesthetic for all that. I've also seen a lot of very formal objects recently too. But being from here and now based here, maybe I just don't know how

to describe it other than experimental and all over the place? From my experience, LA/Hollywood is definitely perceived as mysterious based on responses I get when I've had to introduce myself and where I'm from. I hope it's actual curiosity and not people laughing at my aesthetic that I seem not to know how to even articulate…

Chelsea: I doubt people are laughing at your "aesthetic." Thinking more about location, how did it feel to return to LA after being Detroit-adjacent for two years? Is LA recognizable? Does it feel foreign? Or do you even see any changes?

Philip: LA is home. And after being Detroit-adjacent for two years it never felt more like home. A lot of the schools I applied to were for practical reasons and mostly geographically farther east because I knew I

178

wanted a cultural shift. I was only there for two years, but the Midwest and all my peers I met from the region have definitely influenced me for the better, and I returned with a fresh perspective of LA. When I returned it just seemed much more vast and fast moving than I remember and I'm very proud of how involved the LA community is on current sociopolitical issues.

Chelsea: Yea, I definitely get that feel of LA being very sociopolitical, especially when I hear about the numerous groups working to defend their homes and create awareness of displacement. So with that, what have you been working on lately?

Philip: Upon returning to LA I wanted to get back into my practice. After a few months, I started getting back into drawing. I've been working to find alternative outputs for my drawings and and how to get performative elements back into the work. I found zines as great output for the drawing and text works I've been making on paper.

I applied to some residencies like Vermont Studio Center. I ended up going to VSC and loved every minute of it. I was a bit hesitant applying to residencies because for some of my peers in grad school, it was more about application quantity instead of looking what each program actually had to offer. Also I was in grad school for four years, I didn't have the urge to be in that type of environment straight out of school. I think the month I spent in the rural setting of Vermont helped jumpstart so many new ideas and really made me reflect on how much more aggressive and proactive I can be with my practice.

And I am currently working on a collaboration with another artist. My collaborator is handling the script and performance, while I work on props, set, and art direction. We are working on the piece that will be at PAM, a performance space/residency in Highland Park and will culminate at Torrance Art Museum.

Oki Sogumi

+

Jamie Townsend

When we initially conceived of this exchange Oki and I thought it would be fun to talk about the intersection of writing and other art forms. Both of us are poets but are also involved in our respective music scenes: Oki performing in the band Aphid Daughters and me co-running an indie label, 11A Records. What we found, as we swapped emails over the course of a month, was that the relationship between these practices became a springboard into topics as varied as the anxiety of production, growing up religious, and legibility in art.
—Jamie

Sep 16, 2018, 12:17 PM

Hi Oki

I'm thinking about how we started the idea of this conversation with a certain excitement but also worrying about the fact that we're both really busy right now. I know that, for me, being busy helps distract from (maybe in a less than healthy way?) some of the depression and anxiety that seems to hijack my life too often. Lately I've been considering that dream in the poetry world of not needing to work, of having space, time and funds to just concentrate on writing. In a way, I'm not sure if that would work for me. I think the lack of self-esteem and fear capitalism generates may be the source of a lot of this constant need to produce, but it also feels like something else, a desire to find a multiplicity of me in different creative projects. What's keeping you busy right now and does it help in the day to day?

+++

Sep 18, 2018, 9:44 PM

Hi Jamie,

It's late Tuesday night for me, past midnight, I have Korean reality TV on quietly in the background, and thinking about what to read for a little reading tour I'm doing this weekend w/ Lauren Levin. I'm not a very good multitasker, inevitably nothing gets done!
This weekend I went to a wildlife sanctuary on the outskirts of Philly, adjacent to the airport, and meant to write to you about it afterwards but I was so beat from that little walk and the humid stinky air. I often say I'm busy and in the same breath say nothing is going on with me. The regular stuff of life—the reproducing yourself and the people around you, the small conversations with friends and the shit-talking and the meal-making and responding to my mom's emojis on kakaotalk and re-upping my public transportation card—keeps me occupied. Ongoing projects are helpful as structure. I try to take the time I need, slow down, or concentrate time into the tiny ball of the present. But I'm interested in what you're saying about the multiplicity of you in different

projects, which I think is maybe related to the different kinds of time (in part) that one can put into making stuff.

P.S.

Here are some pictures from my walk. :)

—Oki

+++

Sep 20, 2018, 3:14 PM

Hi Oki

I recently switched to a full-time job at the homeless/houseless center I work at in Oakland and have been getting used to sitting at a front desk for hours again after years of working freelance from home. There's definitely happiness in being involved in this organization, but also a struggle in trying to rearrange my schedule after previously setting my own hours. I also have to be socially available much of the day—which, as a secret introvert, can be completely exhausting. However, one of the reasons I started working here was that working from home all the time, essentially having no human contact most of the week, compounded my chronic anxiety and depression.

I am trying to think through what I meant in my last email about a multiplicity of self and it might be this need to engage these various and seemingly contradictory aspects of me, to explore how my life overlaps with others. Some of it is probably due to being raised in New England as an Evangelical Christian. Though I'm not religious anymore I still feel the greatest satisfaction in working with and towards something redeeming (though often I'm not sure exactly what that is). I believe that if we can repurpose the fucked-up, unending labor of contemporary life toward projects of care (small press publishing, community work, writing and editing, spending time with friends and their art) then I feel like the energy reservoir is a little deeper. As I'm saying this, I realize how tired I am, lol—it's about 80 in Oakland and I've got a stinky catbox and a bunch of writing work waiting for me at home.

Tell me about your tour with Lauren—also, I want to hear more about your band Aphid Daughters!

xo

Jamie

+++

Sep 22, 2018, 6:32 PM

I think often what one desires as an ideal atmosphere or life pattern is based on the extremes of what you've encountered in the past. How nice it would be to only be challenged in the ways one can handle, with reality checks that aren't overly harsh but just gently abrasive like a friend with a witty sarcastic comment that cuts to the core but is wrapped in genuine affection! Lol. Well, it's Saturday night and I'm writing to you after packing for DC and NYC. The

kickoff Philly reading was last night, with Lauren and Jasper Avery. I loved it, got a little weepy inside and then I did kind of meltdown much later in the night. My social anxiety seems tangled with abstract worry about "the collective" and how did my contributions add to existing tendencies creating surplus or lack. It's often the impossible things that don't even make sense to describe, but which seem loosely connected to everything, that make me cry. I also grew up in New England, in a religious family (Presbyterian, and I also went to Hebrew school which sometimes confounds people). I want to ask you a million questions about growing up Evangelical in New England, because I always found it strange to be in this religious family and then going to these WASP-y churches which were more about kind of aesthetic formalism, traditions, and small town sociality than the more intensely emotional space that I later encountered in the church.

I like being both lazy and curious, and wanting things all ways. There is real joy for me in following my curiosities through different mediums and modes of expression and living those multiple timelines, while letting the other jars of stuff ferment (getting Korean with my metaphors lol). As with fermentation, your experience needs to be carried on and not just via written knowledge, it's in the hands. You need to know when to push/stir shit up/focus, and when to let go and wait.

One of my jars/timelines: I probably work on music these days more consistently than I do on writing—my bandmates in Aphid Daughters are friends and we live in the same house or close by, & I make music with my boyfriend, Adam. It's built into and helps sustain my social life. I also find making music a lot easier these days because it feels like a really immediate emotional conduit, stripped of a layer of distancing—cleverness, cynicism, etc. Obviously, that can and does exist in music, but I'm an amateur so I mostly deal in catharsis or fun. I turn into a child who screams a lot into a microphone. That limitation feels really great right now. It's easy to feel depleted and tired and not good enough, but I don't feel that way with music. We are learning a lot in our own ad hoc way and the songs we've started to create change through performance and eventually grow up to be what they want to be. I'm curious about what in your life might feel kind of similar, like a thing you "do" but is also really just a part of your life as much as cleaning out cat litter boxes or walking in the woods for fresh air?

ahhhhh

Oki

+++

Sep 27, 2018, 1:49 PM

Hey Oki

I feel like the idea of wanting it all really resonates. Maybe it's got something to do with a certain type of confidence that is very male and very weaponized in our day-to-day. That some people are just given everything they need to float through life with complete and unquestioned confidence in everything they do. I mean, I want to see people be able to live with confidence, it's just that the idea of "confidence" has been so tainted that I think we need some new language to describe it in a way that suggests an embedded resistance. Does that make sense? Idk, I guess also what I'm trying to say is that we should be afforded the right to be proud of our laziness as well.

I think the music world is a perfect petri dish for these types of imbalances and gendered violence. I read an op-ed article recently by musician Raphaelle Standell-Preston talking about gear culture and misogyny (the marketing of TC Electronics "Pussy Melter" guitar pedal and the subsequent violent trolling of petitioners trying to get the pedal removed from the market). I don't know what changes this because in so many ways popular music in U.S.America has become synonymous with dick worship. I'd be interested in hearing what you have to say about your experiences so far of playing shows and the dynamics of navigating these fucked up spaces. Recently I went and saw Lingua Ignota play a show in SF and while a bro-y metal dude completely disrespected her while she was performing, she wrapped him up in her mic cord and screamed lyrics into his face. It was so great to see her flex like that but then it was also like, "yeah, you've got to stand up to this bullshit probably every night of your tour." I can't imagine how energy like that gets maintained.

I think growing up connected to a sense of spiritual life created systems of thinking that have, actually, been somewhat positive as I've gotten older. The church also admittedly is where music became a great love and central part of my life. It's funny to think that I now run a record label with a friend that I met through a home church more than 15 years ago, and that both of us are no longer religious yet have managed to keep a strong friendship and connection around art and even to a certain degree spiritual things. I think I was lucky though, in a way at least. What was Christian life like for you growing up? How did you get out? (lol)

+++

Sep 30, 2018, 5:43 PM

Tour is over! Listening to Lauren read from their book (which examines a lot about whiteness/racism and gender vis a vis family, pop culture, political events, etc.) had me really thinking a lot about my family too.

I grew up in a family that was constantly in each other's presence/space. Privacy was not something that was available unless you very deliberately sought it out. I used to go on six-hour walks as a kid, just meandering in a

187

two mile radius from my house, slowly observing things around me, just to experience something like a private world. As an adult, I revel in my privacy but also always seek communal and social space. Without much deliberation I easily fall into doing things with other people. People talk about "intentionality" but I'm so oriented by intuition, and its always when I move against my intuition that I feel like I've really exposed myself to damage.

I agree with you about confidence—I think often the ways that we simplify practices of boosting (or what's called empowerment) are often still laden with a lot of baggage and gendered expectations, or thoughtful characterization of how that relational space is lived, or without precise critiques of all the systems in which we find ourselves. I just went in for my citizenship interview/tests (I passed) and I felt myself really being tested emotionally—all the ways I hold myself together were being pulled at, questioned, baited, and meanwhile the Kavanaugh hearing had happened the day before—it was a tough space to be in. I try to undo some of what undergirds my confidence while not decimating it.

In terms of playing music, Aphid Daughters' shows haven't been in awful, bro-centric spaces (we mostly play locally so it's easy to vet) and our audiences have been sweet. I do think that when bands get bigger, there might be more aggression pointed at them, like they think you need to prove yourself. We're so new, and have the advantage of surprise, that could be part of the generosity.

I know you have a background in music—I'm curious to know more about that and what your relationship to music/music scenes is these days?

xo oki

+++

Oct 2, 2018, 3:06 PM

Hey Oki

Congrats at passing your citizenship tests! That's definitely a complex collection of feelings, I imagine.

I like that you bring the importance of surprise and intuition. They both come out of this place that is not unskilled but definitely not tied into the sort of manipulative sense of "mastery." I felt really influenced by punk when I was younger because it seemed to privilege raw expression and a fuck you attitude. Though I listened to a lot of Christian rock music when I was in my early teens, I always favored the stuff that was sloppy, fast, and irreverent.

As a writer, I think I've always taken inspiration from those more underground scenes. I like making things and giving them to people I know, to have that interaction where there's something at stake because there's a relationship involved. My friend Nick and I modeled our magazine *Elderly* after publications like *Maximum Rock'n'Roll* and handmade fanzines, as well as underground literary mags like Steve Abbott's *SOUP* and Sara Larsen/David Brazil's *Try!*. In a way, I feel like a lot of the writing world has gotten too academic, self-serious, and detached. Maybe there's more permission in music to establish a language that comes from the materials at hand (especially things like punk, but also hip-hop, footwork, gqom, black metal) and not from some system of affirmation from

189

the outside. But I realize that's also a projection of my aesthetic hopes onto genres and scenes I'm less immediately connected with than the poetry world.

I'm also still pretty involved with music in my day to day. I'm currently running an independent label called 11A Records with my friend Craig. Some of the musicians we've been working with I've know for years, so it's nice to have a sense of relationship again being at the heart of what we're doing. I think there's a feeling right now with Bandcamp and SoundCloud that small labels are potentially obsolete, though in my mind having a network of support is always needed—to help share costs, do promotion, set up shows, etc. Maybe that's the sort of communal thinking that attracts me to these inevitably unprofitable but socially rich projects. Do you think you want to see Aphid Daughters become something bigger? Do you see it feeding into your writing practice or maybe vice versa?

xoxo

J

+++

Oct 7, 2018, 3:12 PM

Hi!!

I can totally see that you had all those models for *Elderly*—I was immediately drawn to the magazine for those reasons. I also liked that it was on Tumblr. I think a lot of people for a while associated me with the bay area poetry scene, which isn't false, but my connection was more to the political scene when I lived there and where I found poetry and "community" that resonated with me was more through Tumblr in 2012-2013.

Aside from problems of the academic models you mention, I also just think it's an understatement to say that academia does not have a monopoly on critical thinking and has a long way to go in terms of political thinking (and, bound by structural limitations, will never go where it needs to go). Nonetheless, there is thought that moves through academia and poetry by way of people being in both and beyond. I guess when I think of it that way, that we are carriers of whatever experiences, jobs, friendships-and-their-conversations, it doesn't appear as just an aesthetic/formal choice we can make or not. Accessibility is a difficult label that will always trace the outlines of what one has access to and then where that took you, what became difficult, alienating. It's too simplifying to say it's individual, when nothing is, but I also don't find conventional wisdom on what's "accessible" very helpful either. It often feels condescending. Anyway, I say all this as someone who did the whole MFA thing and has an academic parent. It's one kind of stomach, and I kind of like thinking of the process of making stuff as going through a lot of stomach and different digestive juices. Otherwise nothing breaks down. Music is one of those stomachs, and I think maybe one that people use a lot to process or just be in whatever emotional space they wanna be in.

I think what I'm bringing to Aphid Daughters is my body. Which carries all the things I've been digesting in writing, and in other ways. It carries a love of performance and trying things out on the spot. And then that body is also writing. My poetry has always been interested in music because I am. And I've been lucky that when I was taught poetry, there wasn't much formal differentiation between poetry and music, and thinking them together was the approach. A lot of my poetry influences aren't "poets" (their medium is/was music foremost). I've been long obsessed with the band Algebra Suicide and Lydia Tomkiw who was also a published poet...I still haven't read the poems but, in any case, her poetry was in lyrics and songs of Algebra Suicide and her perfect combo of midwestern accent with post punk sneering is so fucking beautiful to me.

I love hearing about what you're doing with the label! The work you're doing is necessary. Just because it's possible for people to do self-promotion, doesn't mean that it isn't a lot of work that, like most things, is better done with more support. The whole "well the internet exists/be your own brand" so you don't need this or that is a bootstrap mentality that need not be the ideal. I love that it is possible to put stuff out there immediately or to self-publish. I also truly appreciate the work that goes into running a small press and the work that editors do. I'm currently working with Skeleton Man press, and Aaron Winslow—the editorial relationship is a collaboration, going back and forth with your thoughts and development of the material. Especially in the case with the current chapbook because it was given to Aaron in a raw jelly state, all rough drafts.

I'm really with you on this: "Maybe that's the sort of communal thinking that attracts me to these inevitably unprofitable but socially rich projects." Yep. I think that explains why I do everything. How do you feel like these projects and/or that rich sociality feeds your own writing? I guess even on the level of desire to do it all says so much, but I'm also interested in what connections you might see or what choices you make in your writing, how you put that writing out in the world. And while we are conversing, and because you mentioned talking to musicians, I'd be curious to hear you talk about conversation's role too, or the density of conversations in working on these projects, what is it about just talking that's so great…

+++

Oct 8, 2018, 9:20 PM

Heya

I keep wondering what accessibility means as a state and how it relates to larger issues, who controls public discourse, and how do different groups use specialized language to insulate or confuse or block. Also, what do we imagine other people want to read? I guess the one thing I'm sure of is that there's a lot of ego involved in how we determine these things. I love that Wendy Trevino ends her bio statement "Wendy is not an experimental writer." I think it gets rid of any assumed "difficulty" before her work is even read, and it also doesn't frame the writing as just an experiment. I really believe writing, any kind of writing, has responsibilities (though complex ones) the same way we all have ethical responsibilities toward each other.

So, yeah…conversation is kind of at the heart of my writing and, in a lot of ways, my day-to-day labor. With the label I have to mediate different types of artistic engagement as well as make sure the translation of ideas between mediums is attentive to needs and limitations on all sides. For the newest album we released I wrote something as part of the back cover design. It could be perceived as experimental in the sense there a lot of parataxis and no linear narrative but I definitely wrote it with the hope that anyone could wade around and feel something in tandem with the music.

I recently realized I'd never escape music as a source of inspiration so I've kind of dug into it even harder. I throw a lot of lyrics into my writing because they're such common, shared language it often seems very intimate to have them there. I have a series of poems that are pretty much completely constructed of lyrics, song titles, or album titles, and the people I've sent them to expressed having different emotions emerge from reading particular lines that are from songs they love or are important to them. I want it to become this shared moment, like we're listening together. So yeah, this totally cycles back to creating opportunities for connecting, talking with people around what they're interested in at the moment.

Speaking of, I'd love to hear about your new chap.

xo

Jamie

+++

Oct 13, 2018, 9:36 PM

Hi Jamie,

I'm getting back late from a movie night at my house, "horror spa" which was a horror/slasher double feature plus face masks for all.

I had trouble responding in the usual format, so I had to make a list:

—The biggest responsibility we have with each other, amongst each other, is ending capitalism.

—Writing is a playful place, for spinning out the dreams and nightmares that crowd our reality. For me, the experiment must also be doing it for real. For example, a protest is both an experiment, and doing it for real, and I think understanding that is kind of important. Writing isn't a protest. In writing, the "doing it for real" is what's happening with the audience and what's intertwined with the continuation of life.

—Here's another useless metaphor: We want to burn the house down, the house which is tangled up in vines, the vines are cut down, they bear the shape of the house as well as the ways the vines decided to go. When the house is burnt down, some of the vines are burnt, and some of the vines bear these shapes. Anyway, I guess it'd be cool to burn down the house and then look at these vines to remember that we did that and why we did it.

—The new chapbook is called "no one sleeps alone in the dark." Because I was thinking a lot about what people, creatures, who find each other during bleak times or underground can do together, the circumstances of finding each other, the loneliness of failing to, which also can be the site of recognizing a collective fate.

—I don't have strong loyalties to any aesthetic form, my inclinations are probably more determined by the content, the politics, and to a certain extent, milieus/contexts for the work. I'm often not impressed. Or I am loving it. But it doesn't necessarily fall into clear patterns. That's not a satisfying answer to those who love to guard the boundaries around the things they love. Personally, I'd like to learn to love in a different way—with less jealousy?

—The music business and poetry/publishing are both structurally limiting, actively demobilizing politically. You can look at what then manages to exist in an available form, sometimes many decades later, but it's a small piece of all the imaginings that did happen. I love much of what exists, but also love what exists outside of surviving in those structures.

Xo

oki

Till Krause

+

Margaret McCarthy

Till Krause and I have been friends for over a decade, since we lived in the same messy and exuberant multi-story collective house in the lower Haight in the early 2000's while Till was a Fullbright Scholar from Germany and I was completing my undergraduate degree, both at SF State. When I moved to Munich several years later, Till let me stay in his living room for an unreasonably long time while I found an apartment. He is a journalist, filmmaker and musician, teaches writing and investigative journalism at several universities, and is currently an editor at Süddeutsche Zeitung Magazine, *the supplement of Germany's major newspaper. We corresponded via email.—Margaret*

Hey Margaret,

Thanks for the questions. I answer them on the train to the airport as I am headed for Berlin for a conference. The S-Bahn is packed! So many people are in town for Oktoberfest.

I started a new band last year with my friend Stefan, who is a great drummer. We know each other from Nuremberg, where we played in different bands and we met here in Munich at the gig of a mutual friend's band.

We are a three-piece (Christoph plays bass guitar), I sing and play guitar. We currently go by the name "So So Sorry" or "Sorry not Sorry" (we can't really decide—which name do you like better?). The name has to do with our lyrics. We write our lyrics using phrases from corporate apology letters. You know, like those full page ads in newspapers, when oil companies cause environmental disasters, or the German carmaker VW cheats with its diesel engines. Or when Facebook messes up people's data.

Our idea is: Why write lyrics from scratch when there is such great material out there for us to use? These are carefully crafted letters, which are supposed to sound apologetic, but in fact are just carefully written words that avoid to express any genuine emotions. Big corporations tend to be super scared of the world, especially when it comes to their public image. So they want to be seen as responsible, taking responsibility for their wrongdoings. But most of the time they use some lawyer-speak. Because admitting real guilt and expressing real concern could open the door. So we use sentences and words from these non-apologetic apologies in our lyrics. Sometimes whole phrases, sometimes just words. Because we think they reflect a very human trait: failing communication. Trying to say something, but being scared of the consequences.

The music we play is some catchy, overdrive guitar pop that sometimes makes you dance and sometimes leaves you standing around wondering what to do with yourself.

The night that Trump was elected will stay with me forever. I remember writing a long email to my American friends:

I believe in humanity, reason and the willingness of (somewhat still) young, (sort of) smart, (kinda) well-educated people like us to take an active role to oppose hatred, be political, show respect and love. We need to get of the screens and into the spheres of real discourse, opposition and argument. Show the haters that diversity and global friendships are more valuable than nationalism. I am devastated but full of hope that we can overcome this dark moment. We must not take our worldview for granted. As the great German publicist and LGBT activist Carolin Emcke wrote recently: "Freedom is not something that you have but something that you do."

I, like many people here in Europe, see the changes in the U.S. with great bewilderment. The language of hatred. Conspiracy theories shared by the government. Trump seems to cross every line and nothing happens. He seems to get away with everything. My main thought is: how is this possible? Many Europeans abhor Trump, but right wing ideology is getting more popular here as well. Do we live in a bubble? Most people I know are doing fairly okay. Yet it feels surreal that people who have been profiting all their live from an open society, liberal values, and global economies are now turning against them.

We must not let this happen.

Much love from Munich,

Till

+++

Till, thanks for these answers! I was just thinking about Oktoberfest. I remember seeing an adult father-son duo in matching lederhosen with fresh purple flowers (maybe violets?) in their hats. In general, I didn't experience masculinity showing up wildly different in Germany than I do in the U.S., but the flowers stuck out to me. They were so delicate and pretty.

I'm very interested in your corporate apology band! It makes me think of this podcast episode from *Rough Translation*, where a woman works with these Japanese companies to try to get them to apologize for war crimes. I vote for "So so sorry" for the band name, because I like the repeating sound pattern.

The ongoing affordability crisis in San Francisco is so real and breaks my heart regularly. There's no way the kind of house you and I lived in together could exist or function these days. I used to be able to wait tables three or four days/week and have enough money to pay rent and not stress. That's completely impossible now. Raph and I have a rent-controlled apartment, so we could stay here as long as we like (some people have lived in my building for decades), but as more and more of my friends move to the East Bay, I question whether this is where I want to be. It's harder or impossible to have spontaneous get-togethers with folks who live over an hour away.

This past week, as Congress moved to confirm Kavanaugh to the Supreme Court, I felt such a despair it was numbing. It's a shock that ran along my spine to realize how many elected representatives, how many pundits, how many voters, ultimately don't think that rape matters. And adjacently, that women don't really matter. That's what the process clearly said to me.

Naturally, I reject their analysis.

But your question to me is what we can do to not lose our minds in times like these. I do believe in finding outlets for action, and I believe very much in the power of working locally. I'm getting involved with my friend's campaign for BART Board of Directors (Janice Li is the change we need!), and I want to give more volunteer hours to Syringe Access Services.

I also think it's an ongoing struggle to balance staying informed with giving yourself space to breathe. For me, that means making weird art, both explicitly political and not. In addition to my ongoing work with the SF Neo-Futurists,

I've just started a new found-text remix project, where I take all the words in a single column of a *New Yorker* article, and turn them into a poem. They're not all equally good, but it bends my brain in ways I'm really enjoying. It also gets me out of thought loops ("everything is overwhelming" and "I don't know what to even write right now," etc).

+++

Dear Margaret,

DADA is something worth looking at in times like these. I find it stunning that it also came at times with huge technological developments, mass production and mass consumption, new forms of media and advertising. This also reminds me of times like these, where not only political shifts are changing the world but also the still relatively new online technologies are a constant driver of change. Would Donald Trump be this successful without social media? I don't think so...

One group of people that constantly makes me laugh are the folks from Botnik (www.botnik.org). They use predictive text algorithms to write all sorts of text, from Coachella Festival line ups with entirely made up bands that all sound as though they might actually exist and play at Coachella (like "Paper Cop" or "One of Pig") to actual songs (where they combine lyrics from Morrissey with Amazon reviews of fitness DVDs). I guess what brings me joy is the combination of things that do not fit together but still work out great. One of my favorite places in Munich is called "Alte Utting," which is basically a full-size steam boat that is no longer in use and was put on an old railway bridge and now is a location for drinks and music and art and all sorts of funny ideas. I love this place. Somehow a great metaphor for our existence in times like these: this does not seem to belong here, but let's still try to make the best out of it.

We really do not celebrate politicians as celebrities over here. The only people who I can recall with Angela Merkel signs were refugees close to the German border who wanted to come to Germany and express their liking for her. Even though she comes from a conservative party that I do not support, I think she does a good job by being calm, reasonable, and not easy to provoke. All of which are essential skills for today's crazy world I guess.

Cheers,

Till

+++

I do worry about the turn in progressive/lefty politics to cut people at (what feels to me) the first failure. I read *Conflict is not Abuse* by Sarah Schulman, which talks about this quite a bit, and how in situations of disagreement and conflict, we need to lay a path for repair and possible re-entry into communities. There's a lot of rejection and shunning going on these days (sometimes really, to my mind, viciously). I think it's bound up in the overall climate of desperation and fear, but I do feel strongly that we need to band together more than we need to tear out the imperfect. Yes, people need to learn and yes, people need to do better, but there's a rapid willingness that to me seems to say, "If you don't know, you can't learn." But we're all human and we're all going to fuck up eventually. Do you know what I'm talking about? Is this a thing in your social circle(s)?

I would love to see masculinity change in light of #metoo. But I wouldn't say I've seen it yet. I'd like to hear more from men about what they're learning, how they see themselves and others needing to change. If there was a podcast that was just a different man every week wrestling with how he's internalized toxic masculinity, I would TOTALLY listen to that. Because I really want to understand how we get them to change. Not how the good ones avoided getting sucked in. Not how the really awful ones just don't care. But normal dudes, non-celebrities, who perpetrate the majority of the harassment and assault and violence, how do they change?

In terms of how to make gender equality a fact...I try to move out from under the framework of "equality" and into the framework of "liberation." We can see how "equality" doesn't truly serve us in countless examples, but let's stick with the recent fact of multiple female senators voting to confirm Kavanaugh. I don't want people of all genders to be equal under the current exploitative systems we have. Not how many women are Fortune 500 CEOs, but how do we design an economy that supports all people, regardless of income? I want all people, regardless of gender, to be liberated from oppression. I believe our path lies

in viewing each other's full humanity, in acknowledging how intersectional our struggles are, and in fighting for justice broadly defined, not narrowly achieved.

You will be jealous of my lunch. I had a burrito, from El Farolito on Mission and 24th. Really, I had half of one, leftover from my dinner last night. Mmmm.

+++

Actually this is a key question in Germany right now. I would say that the change is not so much visible, as many refugees are really trying to become part of German society. But of course there are challenges: many young, sometimes traumatized men who came here out of despair or in hopes for a better future are stranded without permission to work, in a sometimes hostile environment, so this is a breeding ground for trouble.

In Munich, a very rich city with a long history of internationality in postwar Germany, it seems to work out rather well, many refugees are finding jobs, learning

German, and some are now, after several years in the country (the war in Syria has caused people to flee their country for more than seven years now), are applying for German citizenship, starting families and have found a home here. The economy is booming, crime rates are historically low (and a fraction of the crime rate in the U.S.). Bloomberg reported that the 2017 murder rate in Germany was less than 1 per 100,000 population, much lower than the U.S.'s 2016 rate of about 5.3 per 100,000.

What has changed is the perception of the refugees. There has been quite a political shift in Germany, as in many Western democracies, towards right wing populist parties. Often, these parties or groups are the most popular in regions where almost no refugees are living. This puzzles me. In Bavaria for example, the state where I live, there have been state elections this past weekend—and the Green party, which is very liberal, pro-migration and for an open society was the biggest winner. In every major city they got the most votes. This is where most refugees are living. The extreme-right party Alternative für Deutschland (the only German party that partly supports Trump) was also a winner, as they will become part of the Bavarian parliament for the first time, but with around ten percent of the votes they will remain a rather isolated minority. And just recently around 150,000 people marched through Berlin to show support for an open society. This gives me hope!

I send you two pictures that illustrate some points I described earlier. One is a campaign poster from the right wing party AfD that kind of shows their somehow twisted political views. One poster says, "Deport migrants," the other one says, "Better work for care professionals." Germany is a rapidly aging society and there are not enough people working in care. So quite a few people say that migrants (who often are not allowed to work here) could become caretakers, but AfD would rather see them deported. Oh well.

The other picture shows the success of the Green Party here in Munich. It says, "A city turned green."

I guess this concludes our little transatlantic conversation…

I miss you and hope to see you again soon. This has been fun! Talking in person is even more fun.

Cheers from Munich,

Till

Dot Devota

Brandon Shimoda

In the summer of 2009, Dot Devota and Brandon Shimoda lived in Baakleen, in the Chouf Mountains of Lebanon, with their friend Abir and Abir's family in a five-hundred-year-old castle built by Abir's ancestors on the rim of a mountain above a fig orchard. Dot and Brandon traveled in Lebanon and Syria, where they gave readings in Beirut and Damascus, and met with poets, including Etel Adnan, Zeina Hashem Beck, Lukman Derky, Jawdat Fakhreddine, Eskander Hibache, Jennifer MacKenzie, and the late Sabah Zwein. The following are excerpts from their correspondence following Brandon's return to their home in Seattle, while Dot stayed in the Chouf Mountains.

Wednesday, August 12, 2009, 9:22 am, Baakleen

Brandon,

Last night I took your suggestion, or as it seems to me, the small inheritances thieved from you, as any plans you might have for me should have been your endeavors too. But I walked the road below the castle, like a single impalement in earth, my body alone in discovery, and always the discovery is. I am without you, but taking notes for you, talking to you by degrees of body temperature, negotiating our collective knowledge, many whom have their hands outstretched. The road beneath the castle ends very soon after it begins—after it curves out of sight, the road splits and leads to two different properties. To the left, a housing compound built of similar old stones, with many cars parked in front. To the right, a dirt road leads to a shack of sorts. I stood for a long time, not confronted with any sort of "choice," except whether or not to go on at all, and by going on I mean taking a couple more steps, in either direction. I stood by a stone wall, a cactus grew to its same height, as if the living thing didn't want to surpass the nonliving thing, as it offered shade and intimacy, guidance and company, something to compare itself to—a model to strive for is also limiting—like a mirror where the reflection is the maximum capacity of the image. How this cactus, a plant most sensitive to its resources—its plot in life—could apprehend the object it grew near, marrying its sense to a wall! How co-unusual it seemed, although, why haven't I noticed this relationship before? It was chilly near the valley between Abir's and cafe, and I thought maybe it was raining. But the condensation was an opaque fog advancing into the valley. This very fog—I found out—was called "the cooker of grapes and figs." How the temperature cools so rapidly at the brink of worst heat and sweetens the offspring in deep purple, pregnant bellies. Prior to walking down, I was talking to Mr. Ward on his patio—he was the only one home and had the difficult responsibility of visiting with me in English. Telling me story after story, which I welcomed, since anytime I responded he couldn't really find any sensical worth. And there probably wasn't. If you can't speak the language of the land, and then someone of the land endeavors to speak your language so that you do not feel outside the land, then you should be talked at, in your own language, and unable to respond, to equalize the imbalance of power. After a half hour, the story about inventing tail lights came out and began like this: "Do you know Ford? Ford Cars?" But he spoke of his old age, as if it was a heavy and restricting armor he had been, suddenly!, sentenced to wear. An hour into our visit, he doubled over and started shivering, severely, and when I went to touch his arm, he excused himself and said, "This happened in Liberia." This morning when I went to see if he was feeling better, he told me it was leftover symptoms of malaria, which Abir says (I'm noticing a pattern) he INVENTS.

The prison cum library is located right in front of the store where we bought our secret, hidden Almasas. On the 2nd floor—bookshelves cling to the walls and climb to the ceiling. Smaller rooms are off-shoots where couples meet in relative unknown among special archives. Everywhere, a balcony—views of more valleys and their captors—invited the wind, with whatever degree of gentleness or violence—sometimes so strong it began to chisel at the shelves, carving out a valley of its own solely for contemplation and study. But the books made no sound, sat so still, except when Cecilia from Ethiopia was wiping their spines with a rag. After only an hour in there, I felt weathered, wizened, made-over, lined in patterns denoting continual gusts in relentless ventilation! Two books were hand-picked for me by the librarians—SUN MEDALS, a poem to American poets, by Abdullah M Bashrahil; and THE FLAG OF CHILDHOOD, edited by Naomi Shibab Nye. The latter anthology, which featured, among others, Iranian poet Sohrab Sepehri and Sharif S. Elmusa of Palestine—both exciting. Otherwise yes, the anthology was strictly uncomplicated, slaying any frenzied and psycho-social imaginations that might be "misinterpreted" as "volatile" or "extremist" by Western eyes and ears. White guilt and racism undoing any unrecognizable depths. They picked the most pleasant and typical even of Tueni, Adonis, and Darwish. Who are these Westerners who are reading poetry? Or, what are these one or two poems being read? It all appears to be very controlled and manageable by our chosen authorities.

Oh Heart, you should be drowning here. Inventing your water-logged lungs beneath

the sun as it is tallying itself on my bare shoulders. I've found a new freckle for every day!

Later tonight, around 5:30 again, I will see if you feel up to another 3-D encounter, however speechless and fragmented become our reflections.

LOVE, Dot
Wednesday, August 12, 2009, 11:15 pm, Seattle

LADY,

incessant dreams today of the prison cum library, the bookshelves clinging to the walls, climbing to the ceiling, chiseled by errant or purposeful wind; books in their silence, books hand-picked by librarians. were these librarians living or dead? i mean, did they enter into your field of curiosity by motivated spirit, or because you approached them, and asked them to enter? did they have anthologies waiting for you, in anticipating the immanence and emergence of young dot through the doors, or did you ask for collections of poems, and THE FLAG.. is what they offered? i imagine a combination of both, and i imagine—or remember—the "Library of Babel":

> Like all men of the Library, I have traveled in my youth; I have wandered in search of a book, perhaps the catalogue of catalogues; now that my eyes can hardly decipher what I write, I am preparing to die just a few leagues from the hexagon in which I was born. Once I am dead, there will be no lack of pious hands to throw me over the railing; my grave will be the fathomless air; my body will sink endlessly and decay and dissolve in the wind generated by the fall, which is infinite. I say that the Library is unending. The idealists argue that the hexagonal rooms are a necessary form of absolute space or, at least, of our intuition of space. They reason that a triangular or pentagonal room is inconceivable. (The mystics claim that their ecstasy reveals to them a circular chamber containing a great circular book, whose spine is continuous and which follows the complete circle of the walls; but their testimony is suspect; their words, obscure. This cyclical book is God.) Let it suffice now for me to repeat the classic dictum: The Library is a sphere whose exact center is any one of its hexagons and whose circumference is inaccessible.

i wanted to be in a prison library today, but maybe was more so in a library prison, or a prison library after all. my body feels the ache of a different kind of silence, one in which the shedding of light upon the semi-succulent leaves in the throes of silence outside any number of windows, is the precision of silent living that is NOT the living silence of a day as wide and white as the sailing overhead of a whale. this is a silence that becomes marrow in the bone, and my eyes are aching also, from considering the nature of things not exactly too intent- or intensely, but not enough so. i went for a walk in the middle of the afternoon, to find something akin to your library, and even your balcony, and looked out at the islands forming themselves in the air, and the land bridges, and steel bridges, suspension bridges; small trees, dented trees, new build-ings, broken sidewalks, dumpsters overflowing with unrisen sourdough; a white woman sitting on a bench, eating yogurt. so many younger people with red or reddish hair, wearing backpacks, and crossing the street responsibly at the crosswalk—walking with looks of bemusement or feigned ecstasy or otherwise looking vaguely inbred in their americanness, in their plainness. a swarm of chinese men standing before a hot dog vendor, chattering beneath the blue and yellow umbrella, all of the men wearing suits, and carrying attaché cases. people drinking coffee everywhere, in oversized paper cups; women with short, spiked hair in the back; people who cut their sideburns to high level with or above the tops of their ears. i wanted to be lost in an interior pattern, for how-ever much i am always, more or less, lost in an interior pattern. i wanted open windows—tall open windows—and balconies. i wanted to slice into the folded thin brick of halloumi cheese. a man with a metal detector down by the bocce ball courts on fairview avenue. three, fat women smoking cigarettes on a bench, beside a half-barrel planter of purple geraniums. an old lady with tufted, round-ed, yet hollow, reddish hair driving in a minivan down an alleyway and running over a wooden futon frame. young men with green t-shirts; people waiting for a bus that crumples accordion-like or slinky-like into the suggestion of a seawall. many people, many types and gripes of people, on my walk. the nervously tall and slender german man, with the (sort of) flat top haircut, severely creased khaki pants, and an overly patterned, dark-threaded sweater. oh the people, oh the americans. the seagulls shower the people with affections—many trumpets of affections. and then the men diving clumsily off the rocks off the edge of the corniche, in beirut—and the strata of rocks like travertine steps or layered cake. and only men on those rocks—did we ever see a woman among those men? women were swimming at the swimming clubs only, it seemed.

and with the prison library or library prison, i imagined it also buried at the bottom of the square-walled pond in abir's driveway—where the fish loiter at the surface, and then disappear, without warning, down to where? down to the library at the bottom! i think that further, further down, the pond opens up into a room, a room lined with bookshelves clinging to the walls, climbing even further down into the earth. fish don't read, they brush against the spines of books, and feel the content through their scales, cells of words through their shutter-ing gills. what kind of fish are they? orange scaled, with formerly rabid, now algae-deadened eyes.

my entire body aches. i am going to wrap myself in blankets and sheets, in dreaming that you are wrapping me, enwrapping me. that we sleep and dream side-by-side, that we manufacture libraries as we enter them, and disappear them when we leave, together, and without even speaking, is magic, and fortune. all the aches depart, in those moments. if my night is your day, if your night is mine, then we are turning our dreams over and perpetually always, together, for each other. i hang on your every word, for the sun says so, it tells me!

BRANDON

Monday, August 17, 2009, 7:27 am, Baakleen
Brandon,

From the balcony of the library prison, the gap is translucent enough I'm able to see directly to the Mediterranean. But I'm often confusing some smear in the distance for the spectacle of sea, as yet another uninhabitable option. And looking at the sea from an incline---an obtuse point of reference, because really, who is actually of greater height here---it is fat, takes more than normal its portion of horizon, rises vertically although it really extends horizontally, or rather cylindrical, so at the same time you are gaining distance, the outcome would be to return exactly to the departed thing, and the illusion---how something extends in order to escape from us, inflates the lungs and stands tall while retreating, occupying superior portions of space when they are away from us. Sitting at a prison desk, among human idea, our legacy, books---minds condensed and manageable, yet the gaps terrifying. I never want to bind a book again---instead I'll leave pages without numbers loose beneath an open window. Imagine the library then! The white flurry and fury of dried ink. Not the sound of a book laid open (like a game of delicate dominoes). But of albino bats in a sun cave, perpetually crazed and circulating, their restless authors on each page, ghosts the size of many small wings. Books, even they are suspect in this prison---as anything existing within a confine of deadbolts---has been punitively serviced---a maintenance requiring the better parts of some people's lives. Just think of how many wardens spend more time inside a prison than convicts serving a term!

Malika put me back in Haldun's room last night, after having slept in little Riana's bed the night before. It felt like returning to an upstairs room in my grandmother's house, Dot's. (One time I asked Riana what her last name was, she replied: "The life of my grandmother and grandfather is Richani.") A skeletal bed centered in a museum of stacks, old things that are not mine but I feel a familial comfort among. In this castle, I've been switching life-terms. First, piously in the temple, and then as the unmarried grown son, and then as the fatherless daughter (I slept easily that night). My dreams enact and reckon these scenarios---mismatching biographical events, as if reaching a hand into the library turned lottery chamber (where to catch any order of pages would make a winner). And to have a dream is to have taken the chaos and given it gravity, causes and effects, organized and condensed, make coherent the 26 years. The dream assesses its resources and will make due of any amount of displacement and loose change---the transformation is completely inaccurate and recognizable. Like last night's---I walked out of a friend's house from gradeschool, but the friend was not there only his mother, she had been the only parent who ever directly questioned me about the sanity (and sexuality) of my father, as a recovering addict herself, and in the dream I thanked her for her shelter and then she ran to catch me a bus on Jackson street, in the direction of Leschi, knowing I had had a long day clinging to a tree sprouted from the steep cliff of a snow-packed mountain, where I would not dare move because the entire mountain might slide to the valley floor. A chance I couldn't take. Although my life seems to be frequent, small exchanges of chance---a sort of "haphazard commerce" as you once described the main street of Bakleen. Although chances that weren't really a series of grave risks, but instead constant agitation, self-derailment, not because the tracks were rickety but because the tracks were not, I could no longer feel them beneath me---so the new circumstance was "change," but circumstance nonetheless.

Outcomes are always derogatory, too much so for my taste. A malfunction absolute. To have ridden all of those lives to their outcomes would have been a sort of cruelty. Or, to have ridden all of those lives of their outcomes, not bearing witness, equally cruel. Fear with a tail. So to live as I am trapped---and we are---any disproportionate sense of freedom is an illusion one is guiltily greedy of---

I woke in the middle of the night---right as I was telling my brother over the phone that he should not smoke because I could smell his breath through the receiver---and when I woke someone near my window was actually smoking a pipe with cherrywood tobacco. As if they were using my window as a filter between consciousnesses, and when they were exhaling I was catching a dream on a stranger's breath.

Brandon, my body is separating---free-associating particles---to which I must take a side or commit to vapor, that nightly occurrence is darker and heavier than night, should small gestures of light not find ways to penetrate---

I love you, I hope nothing worries you----

Friday, August 21, 2009, 2:12 am, Seattle

LADY,

i am paying attention to the quiet of the night—i am paying attention to the night. i am paying attention to nothing, and therefore i am bleeding out into everything. i am spreading. i am incredibly inefficient, as a bleeding, spreading being, for being bled, and spreading. the tiger leaves are pressing against the window the way prisoners press against the bars of their cages at the arrival of a lone emperor, or maybe a lone, and robed, spirit, removed temporarily from a jade enclosure, or from its body of jade—to parade before them without mission—now floating along, now sitting silently, anyway, upon a golden pedestal, with hair wound into volute forms, as snails moving in circles about the scalp, but not before being dipped in soluble jade; the prisoners react to the open space outside of themselves. i am thinking about the night. the white lily on the table, which was here when i re-arrived from you and from you and lebanon, is now dead, though the solomon swords of its leaves have yet to be de-sugared—that is, informed; the petals of the lily are curling inward, browning slightly, though whether by the seizure of the ochre anthers, and the pollen of the ochre anthers, or from age, from sun cutting over the ears of the prisoners into the room, is not clear. instead, beside the crooked stem, and the flower in descent, a stack of books, and small triangles of color—paper and paper, and the paper of each petal joining the paper of the immediately remote. some things possess themselves at once—some things make the most consoling kind of sense when met late at night, or even more so, not at all. i have been thinking about your prison library, and the libraries inherent in places that cannot be seen—the library at the bottom of the well in abir's driveway, the library behind the leaves that are pressing themselves as prisoners, the library in the back of the refrigerator; the library in each thread, and bag; the library within the couch—the "library" in notre musique. the library in saratoga springs, new york,

210

where i used to sit by the window, overlooking the swales of orange leaves, and read loneliness poems—poems of loneliness—after having spent the entire day inhaling oil paints and turpentine, linseed oil and industrial soap. that is precisely how come, and that is for nothing. i read about animals with enormous ears, i read my way into FLOW CHART, i read my way through anger, and a head permanently—or seemingly—baffled by the backdraft of each sentence, if not word. i was wearing the worst of all possible outfits to fend off the flames and fumes of what became, instantly, something unhandily emitted. i was there, and i was among books. they are not frills, as facetiously said. and now i am listening to the night, the occasional car on 32nd street, the otherwise puritan purse of 32nd street, evolved by sweets and halos and nooses to be a street that hides its perfect harms within the petals of LIVING flowers. there is a wind among the prisoners—the kind of wind that reminds me of being half asleep in an open-window cabin on the pacific coast of a mismanaged, for being tropical, country—but also on the caribbean coast, or the gulf coast, or the coast of cape fear, and the elimination of all daytime distractions, by the wind. i am paying attention for what—because it has to be, and it continually only has to be—meaning that it should be, and it feels like there is absolutely no end to being tired, and no end in resolving to be less so, though without any recourse to actually surmount the problem, not even climbing inside of it, which is a kind of inventive coma. the wind just moved across the back door, though everything is morbidly still. i just drank a glass of pineapple juice, following a glass of lemonade. i must bring things out of other things, in order to have a place to fall back into myself—myself a thing. there is an orange scarecrow in the corner. there is a snake standing straight on the end of its tail. there is the picture window in the front room, and there is really, really wind. paying attention, then, is paying the substance of what is, to pay itself back in the form of being unconditionally. rilke thought endlessly about the immanent LAW of the self, whether the self within or without works of art, or more simply—while others (gibran?) dwelt more fully in the "pattern" of love, as a substance, at least. i am paying attention. i am dreaming of, and dreaming to, bringing and bring you close to me. i am dreaming. the weights embedded inside my body, have both released, and re-doubled, themselves; i am extinguished, again, and i love you —

BRANDON

BAMPFA

Art Lab

Archives

The BAMPFA Art Lab is an art making space that supports visitors in working with a variety of materials during it's drop in hours, and frequently hosts artist led workshops and performance events. One tradition of the space is to side-step the standard institutional modes of communicating with the museum audience by creating hand made mail to send out to an ever-growing mailing list. The only way to get on the mailing list is to send the Art Lab a piece of mail. This small but potent gesture of reaching out to the space through the mail forever binds us to you in continually sharing a strange variety of postal transmissions. The mail the Art Lab sends out is a mix of risograph flyers for events, newsletter compilations of visitor responses to a prompt, political poster art, or often just random pieces of art left behind in the space.
For this New Life feature, we dug through the bountiful archive of mail that has been sent to the BAMPFA Art Lab and chose to scan a group of letters that were sent from out of the area and many from out of the country (Estonia! Jordan! Japan!), to celebrate the connective power of the envelope instrument. Come visit us Thur 4-7, Fri 4-9, Sat 11-9, Sun 11-7, or send us some mail (BAMPFA Art Lab, 2120 Oxford St, Berkeley, CA 94720), and we'll love you forever.

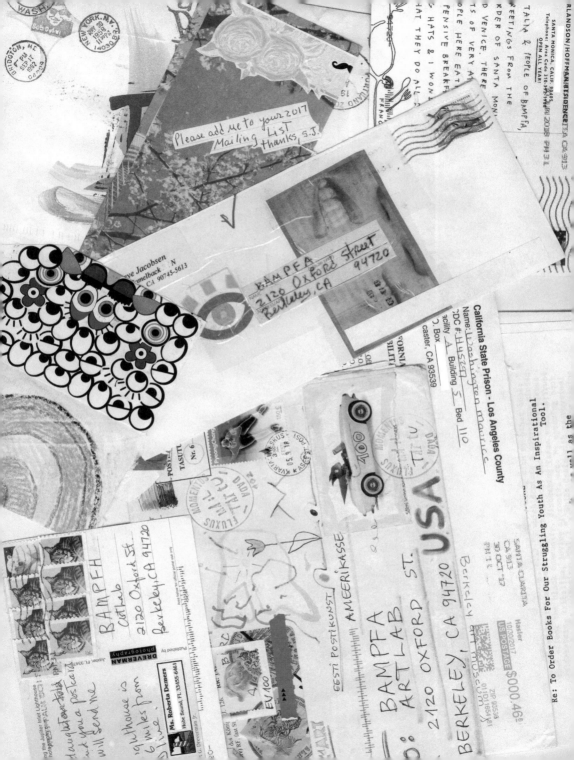

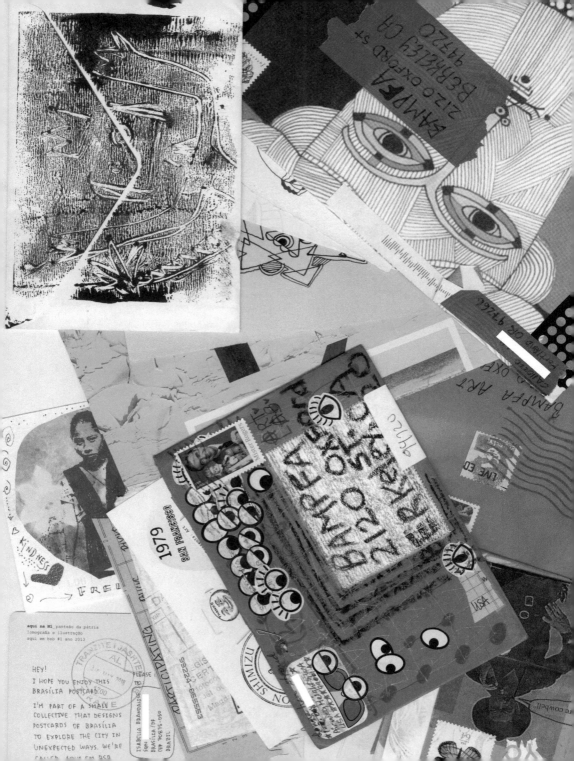

BAMPFA
ZIZO OXPGAD s+
BERKELEY CA
94720

BAMPFA ART

BAMPFA OXP

aqui na BI_ panteão da pátria
lomografia e ilustração
aqui em bsb #1 ano 2013

HEY!
I HOPE YOU ENJOY THIS
BRASÍLIA POSTCARD!

I'M PART OF A SMALL
COLLECTIVE THAT DESIGNS
POSTCARDS OF BRASÍLIA
TO EXPLORE THE CITY IN
UNEXPECTED WAYS. WE'RE

1979
SAN FRANCISCO

KINDNESS

FREE

USA

LIVE ED

ISABELLA BRANDALISE
SQN 403
BRASÍLIA/DF
BRASÍL.
70835-050

Contributors

Andrea Abi-Karam is an arab-american genderqueer punk poet-performer cyborg, writing on the art of killing bros, the intricacies of cyborg bodies, trauma & delayed healing. Their chapbook, *THE AFTERMATH* (Commune Editions, 2016), attempts to queer Fanon's vision of how poetry fails to inspire revolution. Simone White selected their second assemblage, *Villainy* for forthcoming publication with Les Figues. They toured with Sister Spit March 2018 & are hype to live in New York. *EXTRATRANSMISSION* [Kelsey Street Press, 2019] is their first book.

The BAMPFA (Berkeley Art Museum and Pacific Film Archive) Art Lab is an art making space that supports visitors in working with a variety of materials during its drop in hours, and frequently hosts artist led workshops and performance events. The BAMPFA Art Lab in its most recent form, was founded by David Wilson in January 2016.

Kwame Boafo is a performance and movement artist who explores the body as a vessel that archives both public and private memories and (re)members traversed spaces making it the sole narrator of lived experiences.

Claire Boyle is a San Francisco-based writer and the managing editor of *McSweeney's Quarterly Concern*.

Ana Karen G Barajas (1990) is a Mexican graphic designer, artist and art researcher. She was born in Mexico city and lives in China. She studied Graphic Design and a Master in Art at the University in Guanajuato. Her late work focuses in collaboration with people with mental illness and functional diversity. She collaborates in the academic Magazine Bric-á-Brac.

Mitsuko Brooks received her MFA in Painting and Drawing from UCLA, and B.F.A. from Cooper Union For the Advancement of Science and Technology. Brooks is a member of The Asian American Women Artists Association and attended The Oxbow School in Napa Valley, California. Saatchi Art selected her for their 2017 Invest in Art, which was featured in The New York Times and The Los Angeles Times. She completed artist residencies with The Queens Museum (2016) Set on Freedom Artist Retreat; The Wassaic Project (2014); The Snug Harbor Cultural Center & Botanical Garden (2012); and The School of Making Thinking (2013). Brooks was awarded grants from Common Field, The Sally Van Der Lier Fellowship, the Artists' Fellowship, Inc., The Bette Midler Scholarship, and The Resnick Grant. She has exhibited internationally and nationally at The San Francisco Art Institute, California College of Arts, SOMArts, Smack Mellon, Materials for The Arts, Wayfarers Brooklyn, Rush Arts Gallery, and The New Wight Gallery. Brooks' artist books, zines and mail art collages are in permanent collections at Smithsonian's Archive of American Art, Canada's Artexte Information Centre, Barnard College's Library and The Los Angeles Contemporary Archive.

Barbara Browning is the author of three novels: *The Gift* (2017), published by the Emily Books imprint of Coffee House Press, *The Correspondence Artist* (2011), and *I'm Trying to Reach You* (2012), both published by Two Dollar Radio. She has a PhD in comparative literature from Yale University and teaches in the Department of Performance Studies at the Tisch School of the Arts, NYU. She's also a poet, a dancer, and an amateur ukuleleist.

Claire Buss is an award-winning filmmaker making art in Seattle. She is the host and head writer of a nihilist, interactive game show called *The Future is 0*. Claire currently works as a producer and director at *Cut.com*

Sophia Dahlin is a poet in Oakland, where she teaches with California Poets in the Schools and conducts generative writing workshops at E.M. Wolfman. Her work has recently appeared in Fence and the Poetry Foundation's PoetryNow series. With Jacob Kahn, she edits a chapbook press called Eyelet.

Amanda Davis is an interdisciplinary creator and producer working in New York City. She routinely is found obsessing over nuance and performative gestures.

Davey Davis writes about culture, sexuality, and genderqueer embodiment. You can find their recent work at them., Literary Hub, and *BOMB*. Their first book, *the earthquake room*, was released by TigerBee Press in 2017.

Dot Devota is the author of *The Division of Labor* (Rescue Press), *And the Girls Worried Terribly* (Noemi Press), and most recently, *Dept. of Posthumous Letters* (Argos Books). She lives in the Sonoran desert, where she is finishing a book of autofiction called *She*, about a woman who has no reason for anything she does.

Heather Dewey-Hagborg is a transdisciplinary artist and educator who is interested in art as research and critical practice. Her controversial biopolitical art practice includes the project *Stranger Visions* in which she created portrait sculptures from analyses of genetic material (hair, cigarette butts, chewed up gum) collected in public places. Heather has shown work internationally at events and venues including the World Economic Forum, the Daejeon Biennale, the Guangzhou Triennial, and the Shenzhen Urbanism and Architecture Biennale, the Van Abbemuseum, Transmediale and PS1 MOMA. Her work is held in public collections of the Centre Pompidou, the Victoria and Albert Museum, and the New York Historical Society, among others, and has been widely discussed in the media, from the New York Times and the BBC to Art Forum and Wired. Heather has a PhD in Electronic Arts from Rensselaer Polytechnic Institute. She is an artist fellow at AI Now, an Artist-in-Residence at the Exploratorium, as well as Science Center, and is an affiliate of Data & Society. She is also a co-founder and co-curator of REFRESH, an inclusive and politically engaged collaborative platform at the intersection of Art, Science, and Technology.

Chelsea A. Flowers is an artist who holds an MFA from Cranbrook Academy of Art. And a BFA from Denison University with a concentration in Black Studies. She has shown work at various galleries in Columbus and Cleveland Ohio; including Marcia Evans Gallery, Junctionview Studios, with upcoming exhibits at Muted Horn Gallery and ACRE Projects Space. Additionally she has held performances at Hatch Gallery in Detroit, and the Museum of Human Achievement in Austin. She has given performative lectures at Cranbrook Academy of Art, College for Creative Studies and Wayne State University. She has expanded her skills and research by attending ACRE and Unlisted Projects residencies, culminating in various performances at the establishments. Her practice explores subversion to popular culture and how "otherness" is created, and social and cultural critique of her environment. She explores these ideas through comedic troupes, physical play, nostalgic memorabilia, and participatory performance. She is based in Detroit.

Leora Fridman is a writer and educator based in Oakland. She author of *MY FAULT*, among other books of poetry, prose and translation.
More at *leorafridman.com.*

Jasmine Gibson is a Philly jawn living in Brooklyn. She spends her time thinking about sexy things like psychosis, desire, and freedom. She is the author of *the Drapetomania* (Commune Editions, 2015) and *Don't Let Them See Me Like This* (Nightboat, 2018).

Ra Malika Imhotep is a black feminist writer from Atlanta, Georgia currently pursuing a doctoral degree in African Diaspora Studies at the University of California, Berkeley. Her work tends to the relationships between black femininity, aesthetics, and the performance of labor. She is the co-convener of an Oakland-based experiential study group called The Church of Black Feminist Thought and a member of The Black Aesthetic.

Hannah Kingsley-Ma is a writer, radio producer, and infrequent bookseller. Her work has appeared on the CBC, KCRW, KALW and in *Joyland*, *Literary Hub*, and *The Rumpus*.

Philip Košćak is a multidisciplinary artist based in Los Angeles, CA. Who holds a BA (2012) and MA (2015) from California State University, Northridge, CA. along with an MFA from Cranbrook Academy of Art in Bloomfield Hills, MI. (2017). Košćak has shown work in various cities throughout the United States, including Los Angeles, Santa Monica, Indianapolis, and Bloomfield Hills. And has recently completed a residency at Vermont Studio Center.

Till Krause is a journalist, filmmaker and musician from Munich, Germany. While spending three semesters as a Fulbright Scholar in the Bay Area from 2005 - 2007, he learned some important lessons: living with 14 other people can be amazing; digital Capitalism can be quite painful; you can write songs about absolutely everything. He holds a PhD in cultural studies, spoke at Defcon 2018, teaches writing and investigative journalism at several universities and is currently an editor at Süddeutsche Zeitung Magazine, the supplement of Germany's major newspaper.

Nicole Lavelle lives in Northern California. She works with people, place, paper, language, and landscape: her research-driven, project-based social practice yields experimental essays, visual narratives, tools for inquiry, and platforms for participation. She is a Resident Artist at the Prelinger Library where she co-organizes PLACE TALKS, a lecture series about location. She is a former Graduate Fellow and Affiliate Artist at the Headlands Center for the Arts, a freelance visual designer, and a sometimes-instructor of design and research at Portland State University.

MI Leggett is the non-binary artist behind Official Rebrand, Inc. Their work includes but is not limited to: fashion, installation, photography, video & performance. They graduated from Oberlin College with high honors in Studio Art and showed at New York Fashion Week and Art Basel Miami immediately after. They live and work between New York and Berlin.

Julio Linares is an artist from Toledo (Spain) and founder of La Guarida artist's workshop. He has received fellowships from the Council of Toledo and from Matadero Madrid, among others. In 2017 he painted murals at the I Festival Internacional de Mural Inca in The Sacred Valley, Peru. Recent exhibitions and performances include Alimañas estivales, at Diwap Gallery in Seville, and Suga, a performance piece in collaboration with Sepa and Lara Brown that took place at CA2M, Madrid.

Margaret McCarthy is an ensemble member and Co-Artistic Director of the San Francisco Neo-Futurists, and the First Female President of the United States. She has performed at Artists Television Access, Klanghaus, and the Yerba Buena Center for the Arts. More at *unrulyidiom.com*

Vreni Michelini Castillo (a.k.a Chhoti Maa) is a multidisciplinary cultural producer with 11 years of experience; working through art, performance, cultural organizing, music, red medicine and traditional Mexican danza. Much of my work is rooted in Mexican oral tradition, specifically Grandma's storytelling magic. As part of the post-NAFTA diaspora, I was formed by my migrant experience. My work reflects decolonial living, contemporary Indigenous spirituality, queerness, migrant empowerment and the reconstruction of the womyn temple.

j.j. Mull is a poet and bookseller who has lived in the East Bay for almost a decade. He currently manages Alley Cat Books in San Francisco.

Thanh Hằng Phạm is a media maker of words and sounds. She works across radio, poetry and zines. She has produced radio documentaries, Remotely Intimate and We Weren't Born Yesterday and loves running radio workshops for those most underrepresented in media. Under her pen name, Xen Nhà, her writing has appeared in *Peril, Hoax zine, Vănguard zine, Thank You for Nothing* and more. She sees radio as a form of relating, reaching home and healing community. *Xennha.com*

Yosefa Raz's poetry, translations, and essays have appeared in *Entropy, Jacket2, Guernica, The Boston Review*, and *World Literature Today*. She is currently an Assistant Professor in the Department of English at the University of Haifa, where she teaches and thinks about prophecy, apocalypse, outsider art, and the poetics of American bodies.

Kate Robinson Beckwith is a writer and intermedia book artist living in Oakland, CA, where she publishes poetry as Dogpark, runs the Sponge reading series, and makes artists' books as Manifest Press.

Dorothy R. Santos is a Filipina American writer, curator, and researcher whose academic interests include digital art, computational media, and biotechnology. Born and raised in San Francisco, California, she holds Bachelor's degrees in Philosophy and Psychology from the University of San Francisco and received her Master's degree in Visual and Critical Studies at the California College of the Arts. She is currently a Ph.D. student in Film and Digital Media at the University of California, Santa Cruz as a Eugene V. Cota-Robles fellow. Her work appears in *art21*, *Art Practical*, *Rhizome*, *Hyperallergic*, *Ars Technica*, *Vice Motherboard*, and SF MOMA's *Open Space*. Her essay "Materiality to Machines: Manufacturing the Organic and Hypotheses for Future Imaginings," was published in *The Routledge Companion to Biology in Art and Architecture*. She serves as a co-curator for REFRESH, a curatorial collective in partnership with Eyebeam, the program manager for the Processing Foundation, and host for the podcast *PRNT SCRN* produced by Art Practical.

Paul Mpagi Sepuya (b. 1982, San Bernardino, CA) is a Los Angeles-based artist working in photography. His work focuses on the production of portraiture in the artist's studio as a site of homoerotic social relations, and the po-tential of blackness in the space of the "dark room." His work emerged within the queer zine scene of the 2000s, and was most recently shown in "Being: New Photography 2018" at the Museum of Modern Art and solo museum exhibition "Double Enclosure" at FOAM Amsterdam. His work is in the collections of The Museum of Modern Art, the Whitney and Guggenheim Museums, The Studio Museum in Harlem and MOCA Los Angeles, among others.

Brandon Shimoda is the author of *Evening Oracle* (Letter Machine Editions), *The Desert* (The Song Cave), and *The Grave on the Wall* (forthcoming from City Lights). He lives in the Sonoran desert, where he is writing a book about the ongoing afterlife of Japanese American incarceration.

Oki Sogumi was born in Seoul, South Korea as military dictatorship ended and currently lives in Philly. Her genre-promiscuous chapbook, *No One Sleeps Alone in the Dark*, is forthcoming from Skeleton Man Press, and she is perpetually working on a "sci-fi novel" which ferries itself between the living and dead.

Jamie Townsend is a genderqueer poet, publisher, and editor living in Oakland, California. They are half-responsible for Elderly, a publishing experiment and persistent hub of ebullience and disgust. They are the author of several chapbooks of including, most recently, *Pyramid Song* (above/ground press; 2018) and the full-length book *SHADE* (Elis Press; 2015). They are currently editing a forthcoming volume of Steve Abbott's writings (Nightboat, 2019).

Avery Trufelman is a writer and staff producer of *99% Invisible*, a podcast about architecture and design. She knows that fashion is fucking important.

Jeannine Ventura is co-founder/ co-editor at *Undertone Collective & Magazine*. She's a novice writer & podcaster. She's committed to manifesting compassionate and supportive community wherein our experiences, bodies, & realities are respected and valued. *undertonecollective.com* | @ *undertonecollective* | *@undertonemag* | *@oyenenx*

Mary Welcome is a citizen artist with an emphasis on cultural empowerment in rural and under-recognized communities. She believes in small towns, long winters, optimists, parades, and talking about feelings. Her life-long collaborators include Cabin-Time, Camp Little Hope, M12 Studio, Art of the Rural, Common Field, Springboard for the Arts, and the United States Postal Service. She is from Palouse, Washington (pop. 998).

Emerson Whitney is the author of *Ghost Box* (Timeless Infinite Light, 2014) and *Heaven* (McSweeney's, 2020). Emerson's work has recently appeared in *Troubling the Line: Trans and Genderqueer Poetry and Poetics*, *Bombay Gin*, *Jupiter 88*, *ENTER>text: 3 years*, *&NOW AWARDS 3: The Best Innovative Writing*, *Drunken Boat: Romani Issue*, *Cream City Review*, *Agápē Journal*, and *Hold: A Journal*. Emerson was named a kari edwards fellow, PLAYA fellow, REEF resident, and holds a PhD from the European Graduate School. Emerson teaches in the BFA creative writing program at Goddard College and is the Dana and David Dornslife Teaching Postdoctoral Fellow at the University of Southern California.

Dongyi Wu is an artist and designer who is interested in cross-pollination of cultures and diasporic migrations, as well as investigations of traditions and wisdoms from the past as guidance towards the future.

New Life

Supporters

mills college

MFA IN CREATIVE WRITING
MA IN LITERATURE

SPRING 2019
CONTEMPORARY WRITERS SERIES

2/19
DAVID MARRIOTT

3/5
MORGAN PARKER

3/19
SHOBHA RAO

4/6
CLAUDIA CASTRO LUNA &
RENEE MACALINO RUTLEDGE

5000 MacArthur Blvd, Oakland, 94613
grad_eng@mills.edu
readings always at 5:30 pm in the Mills Hall Living Room, everyone welcome

2019 AWP Award Series Guidelines

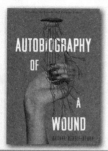

Accepting online submissions Jan. 1–Feb. 28

AWP's Award Series is an annual competition for the publication of excellent new book-length works. The competition is open to all authors writing in English regardless of nationality or residence, and it is open to published and unpublished authors alike.

The Donald Hall Prize for Poetry offers an award of $5,500 and publication by the University of Pittsburgh Press.

The Grace Paley Prize for Short Fiction awards the winner $5,500 and publication by the University of Massachusetts Press.

Winners in the Novel and Creative Nonfiction categories receive a $2,500 honorarium from AWP and publication by New Issues Press and the University of Georgia Press, respectively.

The Award Series conducts an evaluation process of writers, for writers, by writers. AWP hires a staff of "screeners" who are themselves writers; the screeners review manuscripts for the judges. Typically, the screeners will select ten manuscripts in each genre for each judge's final evaluations.

2019 Guidelines

- Manuscripts will be accepted between January 1 and February 28, 2019.
- Submit your manuscript via Submittable at awp.submittable.com/submit.
- For complete guidelines, entry requirements, and terms, please visit awpwriter.org.
- Questions? Email awp@awpwriter.org.

2019 Prizes, Judges, & Presses

The Donald Hall Prize for Poetry: $5,500
Natasha Trethewey
University of Pittsburgh Press

The Grace Paley Prize for Short Fiction: $5,500
Dan Chaon
University of Massachusetts Press

AWP Prize for Creative Nonfiction: $2,500
TBA
University of Georgia Press

AWP Prize for the Novel: $2,500
TBA
New Issues Press

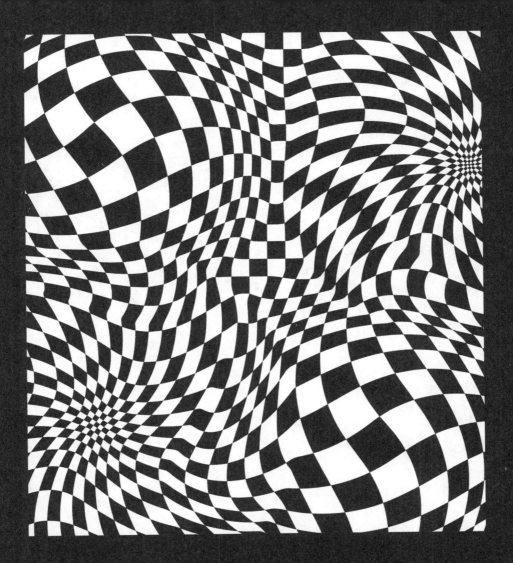

THINGS LOOK DIFFERENT AFTER DARK.

6–10 p.m. every Thursday night at the Exploratorium. Adults-only (18+). **exploratorium.edu/afterdark**

Lose yourself in 650+ interactive exhibits exploring perception, art and science. Grab your friends and a drink and get immersed in mind-bending experiences and unique, thought-provoking programs.

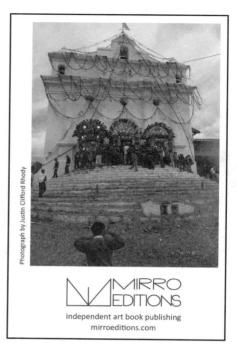

IGNITE

your imagination

ART LAB
Drop in and get creative with local artists right in the museum.

BLACK LIFE
Programmed by Chika Okoye and David Brazil, this monthly multidisciplinary series celebrates the vitality and range of cultural production in the African diaspora. Coming up: Lukaza Branfman-Verissimo, We.Here.Now— She Lives, Amber McZeal.

FULL
If it's 7 p.m. on the night of the full moon, there's a performance going on at BAMPFA. Upcoming performers include PC Muñoz, Hālau O Keikiali'i, and the Chhandam School of Kathak.

WORKSHOPS
Don't just consume culture, create it. DIY art, dance, performance, storytelling, and more.

READINGS
This season, hear from literary lights Norma Liliana Valdez and nick johnson, Marguerite Munoz and Emji Saint Spero, and others.

Details at **bampfa.org**

^^ BLACK LIFE
We.Here.Now: She Lives,
1.26.19

^ FULL
Hālau O Keikiali'i, 1.20.19

UC BERKELEY ART MUSEUM · PACIFIC FILM ARCHIVE
2155 Center Street, Downtown Berkeley | bampfa.org

New from Wolfman Books

Color

Onyinye Alheri

Grace Rosario Perkins

Leila Weefur

Melinda Luisa de Jesús

Jen Everett

Keara Gray

Nasim Aghili

Shylah Pacheco
Hamilton

Celia Herrera
Rodriguez

Lukaza
Branfman-Verissimo

Shah Noor Hussein

EDITED BY
Maya Gomez
Vreni Michelini Castillo

Color Theory brings together womyn
and gender non-conforming working
artists of color from four generations
to explore the intersections of race,
gender, class and labor within
art institutions. The pieces in this
collection engage in an ongoing
dialogue on systemic oppression
and provide a glimpse into practices
of creative solidarity and healing.

Theory